METH-MAN CHRONICLES

VOL III

PETRA

BY

SCOTT CHRISTOPHER

Text copyright © by TC3, LLC 2017
Cover art copyright © by TC3, LLC 2017

Cover Illustration by Jay Carter

Published by TC3, LLC
PO Box 890446
Oklahoma City, OK 73189
MethManChronicles@gmail.com

Printed by CreateSpace, an Amazon.com Company

Dedicated to all of us who think human sex trafficking sucks!!! Oh, and fuck pedophiles too!

Acknowledgement: Thanks to all who helped in the completion of this story. The typist, the editors, the artist, and friends who supported me. A special thanks to those who read the manuscript and provided reviews.

Introduction

You met Petra in "METH-MAN CHRONICLES Volume 1, now get to know her in Volume 3. How did such a beautiful woman become so desperate and highly motivated? In her story, you will get to know Petra before and after her run in with Big Fella and Jimmy. Find out what made her the woman she became and what she did with her "not so fresh start". As her life hangs in the balance, what will she do with a little hope, a little dope, and half a chance? Find out now! This book rocks!

Table of Contents

This is a work of fiction. All names, characters, businesses, places, events, and incidences appearing in this work are results of the author's imagination or used in a fictitious manner. Any resemblance to real persons, living or dead, or to real events is purely coincidental.

PETRA

PETRA

Chapter 1

Staring south out the window of my downtown OKC tower penthouse and remembering, I don't know whether to laugh or cry, maybe a lot of both. Certainly, there was plenty of both when creating the memories in question. I can gaze out and see the whispers of Newcastle gaming center and Riverwind Casino. Ah, all the bizarre and fun and not so fun times there. The Bricktown ball park, I remember before OKC got the expos out of Montreal and the Chickasaw tribe owned the gaming rights to our ball park.

There is the I-35 motel corridor where my first adult freedom began to inch toward its birth. That guy, Garrett, all his friends just called him Big Fella. He was so sweet to me and I fucked him around right after he and his friend, Jimmy Ringo, won my freedom from Javier. What a fucking trip was that night. How many times I had to let a man own me against my will? Many, oh too many. The next morning, however, that would end and I would begin my ascent to this tower downtown here in the heartland. This was the land where I was able to finally give my heart again, to choose vulnerability instead of just being vulnerable.

I lay here in my dusk, not at dusk, but in my dusk. I am about to enter my twilight and what a ride it has been. I look around at this veritable palace, at all the finely appointed luxury that surrounds me now. The bodyguards that are just outside. The housekeepers, the chef, the view, the money. God who doesn't love the smell of money? Who would have ever thought I would be here now, rich, powerful, satisfied and no longer lonely? There she is sleeping, my soulmate, my immortal beloved. Finally, it seems to have all had a purpose. It almost makes some sense. It damn sure was worth the ride.

I sure as hell didn't think this is where this ride would end up that morning, not so many years into the new millennium when I drove away from the Wyndam garden leaving Big Fella forever. He really did not deserve it, especially since he had also just signed over the hot ass generation four Camaro Z-28 I was driving away in. Not to mention the one hundred and twelve grams of methamphetamine that would finance my new start.

I would like to tell you a story. My name is Petra Novakova. This story is my story and I bet you like it. I know I do and I would like it a lot more if I had not lived some of its parts. The new start I was just referring to was the beginning of part III of my life.

I was driving away in that gorgeous red Camaro with a quarter pound of speed that was only just mine because I kind of took it. Now keep in mind this is the greatest amount of personal wealth I had ever had in

my possession at any one time in my life. Also, I had just received the most important possession of all, my freedom. For the first time since I was a twelve-year-old street urchin, I was free!

I was twenty-six that morning. Sometimes it seems like it was yesterday and sometimes it barely seems as though it was even me. Twenty-six and terrified. Twenty-six and elated. Twenty-six and desperate. Twenty-six and finally free. I would never ever not be again.

People in this country take their freedom for granted. Prior to that moment even as a little girl I was never really free, not in Czechoslovakia, Soviet Czechoslovakia.

Anyway, I was driving east through the south side of Oklahoma City not knowing what the fuck to do. I decided I would stop by an acquaintance's place, Melissa, to see if I could sell a little bit of shit and get a room for a night or two and some food. I did not know what would come of that. Right then it did not matter. I just needed to take a hot bath, eat, take a few deep breaths and figure out what my next move was going to be.

While driving to Melissa's place, I began to reflect on the specific series of events that led up to this present situation. Wow, this was one hell of a fucking ride. I still could not quite wrap myself around it. Just a few days prior I had met Big Fella in a dope house. He and I were sitting in the living room smoking a bowl. This guy was obviously into me and he was

huge. I mean like way fucking huge. I was not scared though. He just looked at me like I was something he was seeing for the first time. Not a woman, he surely had seen plenty of them. But a real person he was into and wanted to know more about.

Now at the risk of sounding a little cocky I am still pretty hot. But then I was P.H.A.T. I was owner of a body built for sex, hourglass figure, big full breasts and lips, creamy alabaster skin, flaming mahogany red hair and piercing sultry green eyes. All this combined with an Eastern bloc accent and smoky soft voice. Most men could not resist my charms. I am not too tall, about 5'5". In platform heels I am a show stopper. To quote an American movie, I had him at hello.

Javier, my owner, was in the back room selling some dope and Big Fella was there with this guy that Javier was dealing with. Javier did not keep me under lock and key. The fear of what would happen if I tried to run away was enough. I had been a slave for about fourteen years at that point, so it was what I was used to. This Big Fella wouldn't have any fear at all. It also crossed my mind that I wouldn't be afraid either, not with him. I gave him my number. He seemed really happy about that. As we sat there talking about things in general, there was a show on the television about human sex trafficking. Big Fella got angry while he watched this shit on the T.V. It became obvious that he despised the thought of human sex slaves. That was kind of ironic since this guy he showed up with was

into the slave trade here in Oklahoma and Texas. Obviously Big Fella didn't know about all that.

As the two of them drove off in the red Z-28 it got me to thinking. You know just maybe, just maybe? Javier came out and laughed at me and then asked, "You got that big man reeled in didn't you baby? "We will have to get Marco involved and see if we can't have you get some of his money for me. Now get your ass over here and suck this cock you fucking whore," he demanded.

Javier pulled his gym shorts over and exposed his prick to me and waggled it with his fingers. I crawled over to him and licked my lips at him putting on my best come fuck me look.

"Coming baby! I said to him thinking all the while that this might not be my life for much longer. For now, I would just try to get through this fucking moment. Somehow the thought this might have an end, other than my death, gave me hope; while at the same time it gave me the resolve to do what was necessary to escape this current reality.

After literally tons of practice I was pretty fucking good at giving head. I was mercilessly talented today as I wanted it over quickly so maybe this asshole would leave for a while.

"That's it you dirty fucking bitch. Suck it just like that! "I'm coming! Fuck yes!" Javier exclaimed as he shot his fucking spic wad in my mouth.

I was positive as I wiped his cum off my chin and licked my lips that I was definitely gonna try to turn Big Fella into Captain save a Ho. I knew one thing for sure, I did not want to live like that anymore.

"That was great Sugar. You suck cock better than any other bitch ever. I am heading out. I will see you after a bit. Don't miss me too much."

Chapter 2

What the fuck is wrong with these assholes? Don't they fucking get it? They act like us girls are their girlfriends. WTF? Really? All men have to be fucking clueless. At least all the men since I was a little girl, before the accident. I wanted to scream! If you buy me, I don't love you mother fucker.

Enough of that. Javier left and I called Big Fella up and started to chat him up a bit. It was obvious as hell that this was going to be as easy as pie. The big man was on the hook. We talked for an hour or so. Then I hung up abruptly, acting like Javier had just gotten home. I had hoped hanging up quickly and expressing fear would bring out some of the protective instincts I was pretty sure I sensed in this guy. I could also tell that the broken English I spoke was driving him wild as hell.

A couple of hours later Javier popped back into the house and told me to pack a bag with my bath products and some sexy lingerie and shit. I knew what that meant and twenty-two visitors later I was being driven back to the house after stopping at McDonalds on the highway.

This mother fucker had just made three thousand dollars by renting out my pussy and I got a fucking sausage biscuit, some juice and his dick shoved in my mouth after we got back to the house. This shit had to stop. I couldn't do this shit over and over anymore, especially if I was not going to get anything but his dick out of it.

He left after I got into the bath tub. As he walked out the door he said the same old tired bull shit about my missing him too much and all. Fuck him! I took a chance and called Big Fella up and asked him to come over. I figured Javier would be gone until early evening anyway so I had to make this happen quickly. I was not prepared to have another twenty dicks stuck in me again that night.

I got out of the bath and powdered myself up. I put on some tight short shorts and a tank top that had my tits popping out and my nipples poking through. I was ready to make the hard press and reel this guy in. I felt kind of bad about it. He seemed like a nice guy. He was my only chance though.

I watched as the red Camaro pulled up and couldn't help but get excited about it. It seemed to confuse me. It really felt I had genuine feelings for this man. His appearance even made me kind of wet. I guess looking back now, I probably did have real feelings for him. He represented a chance for freedom. I had been such a good little slave girl for so long now that I did not even remember when it had even crossed

my mind that freedom was an option and here it was walking up the steps.

"Well, hello there, big boy," I said giving him my best come hither looks.

"Hi", he said nervously.

I could tell that my choice of attire had been correct. My toes and fingernails had been recently done and Big Fella was definitely digging the merchandise. I asked him if he had any shit and he responded by pulling a fat pipe with a big bowl on it out of his jean jacket pocket.

"Oh my! It's so big!" I exclaimed as I wrapped my lips around the shaft of the pipe. I moaned approvingly as I sucked in the thick white smoke. By the way, I absolutely knew what I was doing to him. I knew every step of the way what I was doing. My head exploded in a rush of intense pleasure as I passed the pipe to Big Fella and dropped down between his legs.

"Now let's see what the big boy has for me here." I said to him as my finger and thumb found his zipper and opened up his jeans. Pulling down his underwear I smiled at him and stared up right into his unbelieving eyes as I took his rapidly swelling purple mushroom top into my mouth and slowly began to slide my plump lips down his thick extending shaft, slithering my wet tongue in a rocking motion along the underside of his leash.

I knew I had to make sure this was the fuck of a lifetime for him. That was my collar. This was the

most important fuck of my life. Without the collar the leash could not lead him. I had all the confidence in the world. For one I had several lifetimes worth of experience and amazingly I still had a beautiful tight pussy. Secondly, I had a body that was built for fucking.

He pulled deeply on the pipe and I felt his back arch as he exhaled. This thrust his nice cock right into the back of my throat and his hands found the back of my head. I swallowed hard on his shaft and felt him almost give up his nut right then.

I sucked hard as I slowly pulled my lips backwards popping his rod out of my grip and gasping as it sprung free. I let the slobber in my mouth sling out as I stared up into his eyes smiling. I must own this man I thought to myself as I began to lick and suck on his balls. Wrapping my little hand around his meaty shaft and pumping hard and slow, I moved my mouth to the head of his dick. The top was bright purple as I began gently sucking the head and licking that special spot right underneath his helmet's underbelly.

"Oh, fuck Petra. Oh, fuck yes! Please. Oh, my fucking god please!" He gasped.

That was my cue. Severely fastening my lips around his wet prick while at the same time lacing my fingers within his, I forced my head down onto his dick until I gagged just a little bit. He got the message and began to fuck my mouth. Open a little, gag, swallow and then suck hard as he withdrew.

"Oooh myyy good fuck! Aaaaah! He exclaimed after a few thrusts. I felt his shaft swell then pulse followed by his forceful jerking about as long ropey strands of his appreciation flew across my tongue and into the back of my throat.

Determined not to miss a drop and to see that he returns to full mast quickly I never released him. Slowly and gently I nurtured him back to where I needed him to be. When he was once again turgid, I hopped on his pole allowing him to feel my warm, hot, tight pussy. Sucking on and moaning into his neck, I rode him for everything I was worth or ever would be until he screamed and I once again felt the strong pulses of his approval.

We both sat there gasping for breath, glowing pink. Completely satiated, he would obey me. He must for Christ's sake. Christ, dear Lord it had been so long since I felt anything like the hope of redemption. Was this the beginning of my renewal? Here on this cum and sweat stained ugly couch? As they say, "From humble beginnings".

I began to sob as I sat atop him, his tool still in me, listening to him try to catch his breath. He held me as I cried. I really wasn't even acting just yet. I was crying tears of relief, genuine tears of hope.

"What is wrong, Petra?" He asked me.

I launched into a brief rundown of my childhood, adolescence, and how I came to be Javier's slave, his whore as it were. I told him about the night

before at the Bel-aisle motel. The dirty little rooms, the
filthy acts, my shame, my total lack of hope, my
despair. I was truthful when I told him of the hope he
brought me. I was less than honest when I let him
believe why. I was totally honest once again when I
mentioned the night to come, about how Javier had
paid the motel for two nights, about how much I did
not want to be used for sex anymore. I told him about
the last fourteen years of my life.

The trap was set! I was sure he would allow his
natural protection instincts to kick in forcing him to
rescue me. That was the plan anyway.

"Can't something be done?" He asked.

I told him he could just show up and tell Javier
that he couldn't have me anymore and that I would no
longer be his slave. I just hoped Garrett, that was Big
Fella's name by the way, wouldn't have strong instincts
towards ownership after the rescue was complete.

Of course, if it all back fired on me I could
claim Garrett was merely an obsessed weirdo, then
blow Javier's dumb ass and tell him thank you for
saving me. I asked Garrett if he would help me.

He said, "Yes."

Trap sprung!! I gave him my room number and
address. He agreed to come by.

With a little luck tonight, my fortunes would
change. With a little luck? Of course, no imagination
could have prepared me for the evening to come, none
at all. We hung out and smoked a little weed together.

Then we rolled a bowl of shit and I kissed his liberating mouth as he left.

Chapter 3

I went back to the bathroom and showered, powdered and packed my bag for the night. Everything looked as it should look and I waited for Javier to return.

Javier returned with that slimy fuck, Marco. They walked into the kitchen and began to eat some leftovers and talk about me as if I wasn't even there. Of course, to them I was not a real person. I was a blow-up doll and at other times an ATM machine, never though a real live, living, breathing human being.

I could hear Marco indicating that he wanted his cock sucked. I watched and listened as my mouth as well as my dignity were bartered for, bartered for one last time.

I smiled and watched Marco walk out of the kitchen and pull out his little pecker. I wanted to laugh at his tiny, skinny little dick but I knew better. Instead I laughed inside while I sucked him off. When he was through, his cock was replaced by Javier's for the last time.

I smiled and walked to the bathroom. I closed the door and made myself throw up. I spit him up and

out and flushed him symbolically, just like I would hopefully flush him for good later. I brushed my teeth and rinsed my mouth indicating that I was ready whenever he was.

He smiled, slapped me on the ass and told me to go get him paid.

"Go get daddy some money now sweetness," he said.

I was instructed to ride to the motel with Marco. I did as I was told. I listened barely as I was once again insulted as we pulled up.

"Get the fuck out bitch!" Marco said as he stopped in front of the door.

Smiling I walked up to the door to the room and disappeared inside. I almost exploded with excitement as I plopped down on the bed and turned on the television set. I laughed with disgust as the startled cockroaches scurried away. My thoughts raced as the sounds of Maury Povich and his stage full of he-shes could barely be heard in the background. Another trap was set. I had only to wait for Garrett. There would be no Johns today. Big Fella would see to that.

I laid there and checked the door as it was knocked upon. The first few times were expectant johns. I did not answer. As a touch of panic began to set in, there was another knock at the door. It was him. He had come. This plan was going to work. It had to work.

I greeted him with a big hug and kiss. "You came!" I exclaimed.

"Of course I did. I said I would". He responded as if it were preposterous that I had thought he would not keep his word.

That is so odd. We obviously come from different worlds as I had always found it weird if anyone ever kept their word. Trap number two had nearly sprung. The potential johns that I had not answered the door for would soon find Javier and he would come to see what gives.

Once again I could not have predicted what was to happen next. The door opened and the show was to begin immediately. Javier sat down at the table, looked in Garrett's direction and then looked toward me.

"What the fuck is going on here? Why is Big Fella here? How much money have you made? Why haven't you been answering the door?"

I answered by saying, "Garrett wants to talk to you. I, of course, realized I had answered all his questions while also answering none of them."

Javier raised his voice and spoke to Garrett. "Big Fella, what the fuck is this about?" As he asked, he pulled out his revolver and set it on the table pointing it at Garrett.

"Look Javier, Petra won't be working anymore. We are in love." Garrett said matter of factly.

Javier yells, "What the fuck does that mean to me? Don't you understand? She is my fucking

property! You can't just take what is mine you fucking fat ass moron. Thirty thousand dollars. That's the price. Thirty thousand dollars."

"I don't have that much!" Garrett said.

Well this began a silent stare down and after a while Garrett took a call. Not exactly sure how it happened, but I got the impression that someone was coming over that Javier thought would buy me out from him. All of this was surreal and it seemed like it was happening in slow motion and fast forward all at the same time. Then there was knock on the door.

Javier told me to answer the door. I opened the door to a tough looking man who introduced himself as Jimmy Ringo. Within a minute or two Jimmy had Javier's revolver at his own temple and pulled trigger. He then slammed it on the table and said, "Your turn", or some shit.

Next, there was a loud bang and the wall was covered in brains and blood, Javier's brains and blood. The next two hours are a blur. The friend of Garrett's named Jimmy took control of the situation. The cops came and then we all went downtown separately. Then I was on my way to the Wyndam and we couldn't pay. Then this Jimmy reappears, congratulates me on my freedom, pays for the room, gives us some refreshments and disappears.

Later, I would find out that he and his pal, Big Fella, were really about something and ended up doing ok for themselves after a few bumps in the road. Either

way that night I was stuck with a six foot three, three hundred fifty pound, love sick puppy that thought we were gonna spend our lives together or something like that.

The truth is I probably would have done well as Garrett's woman, but after a fourteen-year run as a sex slave, I really wasn't relationship material. What I needed was money and a chance at a new life. I had an ID. I was legal. Javier had taken care of all that, fear kept me and other girls like me in line. Fear and routine is what we knew.

I was sitting there snacking on a deli tray amazed that I had had the courage to believe that I could be free. I was also upset about what I was about to do to this guy who was actually pretty nice. I was able to do it to him by convincing myself he would end up being like all the other men I had known.

I played the role I had to play and got him to sign over his car to me. In return for allowing me to fuck him, I fucked and sucked his brains out. For at least that night this dude had some of the sweetest pussy I ever threw on anyone, and he had it all night long. Hell, I was grateful for what he had done.

Anyway, so here I was driving away in my new Z/28 with the quarter pound of dope I found inside. There was Melissa's place coming up. She lived right over behind the giant green warehouse and always seemed to have a crop of semi-homeless chicks around. It looked like she was home and I got out and walked to the door.

After knocking on the door and waiting for a moment or two, the door opened as I was about to walk away. There was Melissa, a buxom fox, standing in the doorway.

"Hey there, what are you up to girl?" She asked as I walked into the shabby little single level home. The furniture was all retread retro late seventies crap deco, but she was always welcoming and usually needed to score some dope. She had heard about some problem over at the Bel-Isle. She was still freaking out about the whole Javier/Russian Roulette/ brains on the wall thing as I got up and left. She had purchased a half an ounce for four hundred fifty dollars.

I kept heading east and stopped on the I-35 corridor and spent three hundred twenty-five bucks on an extended stay suite for a week. I went to the store and came back with food, a few paper products, a bunch of stuff to drink, some smokes and a meth pipe.

Chapter 4

I ran and took a long hot bath, got out and wrapped myself in a towel and sat down in the lounger. I sparked up a smoke and closed my eyes. I inhaled deeply and watched the memories of my life appear on the back of my eyelids and let the tears come, hoping that they might just wash the pain away or that maybe at least they would christen the new beginning. That just may be the next phase would be blessed.

My mind drifted and there was an image of a cute little red-haired girl. I exhale the smoke and remember that the beautiful little girl is me. I watch as I waddle up toward a picnic table where an adult couple are preparing a picnic lunch. As I remember my parents, Jakule and Kateena, I smile. Two more children join me. My older sisters, Anna and Tereza were already gorgeous young, but school age girls. Anna, a blonde, and Tereza, a brunette, were seven and ten respectively. I was only four at the time. A handsome young man appears, approaching from my viewpoint. It was my big brother, Tomas.

My beginnings were humble but middle class. We lived in Prague and we were having a picnic much like any other working class family. We were four

normal, happy, attractive children with two parents that were relatively decent people. I remember being taught right from wrong. I remember Tomas was into girls and we would tease him. He was two years older than Tereza. He was the oldest and I was his baby. We really were like all those families I barely believe even exist now. Our mother, Kateena, stayed at home. I believe our father, Jakule, did something in the medical field, at least he wore one of those white lab coats to work. I remember that was time like a four-year-old girl or a twelve-year-old boy should have. Simple basic, inquisitive, full of wonder.

Our little split level home on a hill in town was decorated in these bright but still drab yellow, odd oranges and rust. We had a wire haired little brown terrier that spent all its time barking at the gray squirrels in the giant oak tree in back. I remember Anna, Tereza, and Tomas all taking turns pushing me in the tire swing hanging from one of its limbs, and smiling naturally, not as part of an act. I believe I remember being happy, not at all concerned about much of anything and positive that things would forever move forward in this fashion perpetually and unchanged. What I wonder would have become of me had my existence remained unaltered. I don't wonder that often, but sometimes I do wonder that.

We were attractive kids from an attractive family that lived in a cute house. We went to school and got there on time and everything. We celebrated holidays together and got presents on Christmas and all

that. It was Soviet controlled, but I don't recall being unhappy at that time. Looking back to where I was at that moment I am not sure I really believed it had been my life once; family, happy and all that well-adjusted bull shit. Where would my life go from here? This odd, newly free place that had its own batch of fears. For now, however, I was merely content to sit there in that lounger and remember. Those memories would stop. It would not last for our family, the Novakovas.

Three years later something would happen to change everything. Everything! The six of us were all together at a department store near the exit in the toy section. I, of course, am completely and totally into everything around me zipping from this display here to this display there, desperately needing to touch and then take home everything in sight.

Out of the background of noises, I hear my parents telling us, "Kids we are going to get the car. We will pick you up at the door!"

After none of us respond, my father, Jakule, hollered "Tomas, do you hear me? Round them up!" He motioned to the three of us girls.

As Tomas answered "Yes, Father" it never occurred to me this would be the last time I heard Father's voice. As I watched them walk through the doors smiling back at us and then at each other, I was completely unprepared for what happened next.

Tomas got the three of us rounded up and headed toward the exit. As I walked through the first

set of doors, I looked out towards the parking area and saw a man speaking to my father. Then I noticed he had a gun. A gun pointed at my father. I saw the flash leave the barrel and my father fell. I watched my mother's head follow my father's body to the ground and then she turned toward the man screaming. I saw the flame leap from the gun barrel again and heard its rapport. My mother falls to the ground and the man disappears from view, a blur of worn black, overcoat. I begin to scream and am swept up into the arms of Tomas as the four of us shake and cry in disbelief.

As horrible as this moment was, looking back, I had no concept of how dramatically and quite possibly irreversibly life had changed. I was too young to really get it and as I was laying there remembering, I don't think I had it yet. Even now as I sit in opulence, a powerful woman in my fifties, I am still unsure if I understand the gravity of that day.

Chapter 5

At first, things were kind of ok. The four of us went to live with our great aunt Natalie. We got most of our belongings and we were told that we were welcome and would be well loved and cared for. Aunt Natalie's house was nice and we were well fed and she was nice as well. We went to school and we played and I was really doing well with it all. All of us were.

I wondered why I didn't remember Aunt Natalie at all. None of us did. The four of us all thought it very strange since she was so sweet.

We were all aware that there was a husband, our Uncle Karl. We had not seen him yet other than in pictures. They had never had any children of their own. No matter, we were all healing in our own ways and adjusting nicely. Things really seemed like they would end up alright. We missed our parents, but if we couldn't have them this seemed like the next best thing.

Aunt Natalie was a pleasant and proper woman. She could cook very well and seemed to enjoy having us around to parent. She seemed pretty good at it, too. As it turned out, Uncle Karl was away a lot because he was usually in France, Spain or Germany on business. Apparently, he did something for the state, a job

working abroad for our communist government. Nobody seemed to know exactly what, but that didn't matter, and he was never there anyway.

Just before my eighth birthday, Anna and I came in the house from playing in the back yard. There was a large man with a kind face in the parlor with Aunt Natalie, Tomas, and Tereza. He smiled as we entered the room. His smile was as inviting as his face. I liked him instantly.

"You must be Anna and Petra," the man said. "I am your uncle Karl."

I ran and jumped into his lap. The six of us had tea and cookies as we laughed and smiled together. Together there were six of us again and we were together smiling and laughing. He was fun and he read stories to me like "Cinderella" and "Hansel and Gretel." He played tea party and dolls with both Anna and me every day. For almost four weeks I was feeling like life would be getting more and more normal. I was doing well and so was Anna.

Tomas and Tereza both got in trouble about one week before Uncle Karl went back to Western Europe. Separately, but almost on the same day, they had both been reprimanded for being disrespectful to their teachers. This marked the beginning of what Aunt Natalie would call their teenage blues and dismissed it as normal pubescent behavior. What the hell did I know? I was only eight years old.

What I did notice was that while Anna and I were flourishing and really beginning to blossom. Our older siblings were starting to wilt. After they first got into trouble, things seemed to get a little better for a while and then they would get worse. Overall they just seemed to be more distant; more apart from than a part of.

I overheard Aunt Natalie telling one of her friends that she thought those two were on drugs. She was positive about Tomas and nearly positive about Tereza.

I did not understand also that they began to show visibly that they got worse as a visit from Uncle Karl got close. For me I loved it when Uncle Karl came home to visit. He obviously loved all of us so much. He showered attention upon on us all and really seemed to care so much. I really thought if Tomas and Tereza would only spend as much time trying to be a part of this family unit as they did trying to ruin themselves, more of their problems would disappear. Of course, I did not have any clear memory of my day to day emotional state when our mother and father were alive. I was certain I was as happy as I had ever been. I was certain it had to be the drugs that were the problem. It would not be until later that I would learn that drugs were a solution for problems. They may indeed cause some problems, but at first people use drugs to solve problems that seem unsolvable. Too soon my education would begin.

I noticed that when Uncle Karl was home, Aunt Natalie seemed to have more social engagements and consequently would be out of the house more. I really didn't give it a lot of thought until one evening. Aunt Natalie was out at a meeting of one charitable organization or another. She was involved with many.

Anna and I were both excited that evening after supper Tomas was who knew where, but out of the house. Tereza was at a friend's house. Uncle Karl, Anna and I would be having a tea party. It was uncanny how into dolls and our tea parties beloved Uncle Karl was. Anna and I loved it and we loved him. So like I said, we were excited about a chance to have him all to ourselves. We had no idea how mutual the feeling was.

The two of us put on our cutest little dresses and the three of us laughed and had our tea party with our cookies and scones. We imagined that the three of us were all members of an old Prussian court and that all our words were so very important to the peasants that were waiting for a daily report of just how we felt about things.

We had been playing royal tea party for about an hour when Uncle Karl told a joke and laid back on the carpet laughing. The two of us jumped on him and we all three were rolling around. I felt a hard bulge in the front of his pants.

"What's that?" I asked Uncle Karl.

I was certain that this is what had happened to Tomas and Tereza. I felt exactly how they had looked. Within all this pain, that mystery was solved. I went to sleep exhausted, robbed of my humanity, wanting to die. I was almost ten. Almost!

Chapter 6

I remember nothing of my dreams that night, but when I woke up I still wanted death. I felt nonexistent other than the severe physical pain I would have to endure. I had not even healed enough to begin to hurt. The worst was to come.

As I walked to the school bus with Anna, there was no more joy for us; only shame and pain. We must have looked like zombies.

Tomas and Tereza noticed and they rode sitting next to us. No words needed to be said. No words would begin to solve this. No words could cure it. The four of us sat broken, together, yet alone.

I sat there in pain, certain that this horrific experience was exactly what had happened to Tomas and Tereza. I wanted to be angry, but had not healed enough yet to be furious. This was not the case for Tomas; he was furious. I could feel the heat coming off him, although there were no words between us. His arm brought me the only comfort I would get that day.

School was a blur, nothing more. All I learned that day was how to deal with more pain that I previously knew was possible. There would be more to

deal with that day. The bus ride home was an uneventful blur, much like the rest of the day. I still just wanted to die.

The four of us got off the bus and walked toward the house. It was no longer my house. Now it was merely a crime scene where my things were. Tomas had an intensity about him that I had never experienced with any other person. Four broken children walking up the street. We approached the house, went up the stairs and through the door.

"Children, good afternoon. Come to the kitchen." Aunt Natalie hollered at us through the house.

There was the wonderful smell of fresh baked cookies, but, this time, it brought no joy to children. We walked into the kitchen and there was Uncle Karl.

"Hello kiddies. How was school today?" He asked.

I stood there in disbelief. There was the same friendly voice, the same ultra-pleasant face that had always been there. Now, however, I realized that I had been staring at a sociopathic lunatic.

Aunt Natalie turned to us with a large plate of brown sugar, oatmeal, raisin cookies and a big smile. "Tomas, did you and Tereza stay out of trouble today?" She asked.

I remember looking at her, knowing what I would later learn was appalled. She knew. She had to fucking know. She was a psychopath as well. They both were. This is absolutely diabolical. I thought

about how Tomas and Tereza must have suffered. I
thought how brave they had been. How hard this time
must have been for them. I thought about the times I
had overheard conversations from the church ladies
about the children Uncle Karl and Aunt Natalie had
fostered before. How long had this song and dance
gone on? How long would it continue? How would I
make it through all this? Would I have to endure this
for eight more years? Could I?

The other three kids, my brothers and sisters,
even through all their pain, were able to continue the
charade. They approached Aunt Natalie and each got a
cookie.

I instead screamed, "No ooo ooo!" At the top
of my lungs I screamed and did not stop screaming.

Tears were shooting outward from my eyes. I
was gasping through sobs and screams. This couldn't
go on. I was turning ten the next week. I couldn't
endure this for eight more years. I was not as strong as
the other three.

"No, no, no, no!" I heard myself babbling
between sobs.

Tomas shot over to the counter and grabbed a
knife from the butcher block. He was turning towards
Uncle Karl and yelling, "You son of a bitch. You
promised! Not the little ones!" He jumped hitting
Uncle Karl in the chest. The two of them fell as the
chair collapsed from the impact. There was blood and

then the sound of suction from the knife as it was yanked from Uncle Karl's chest.

Splatters of blood across my face were warm. I was now silent.

Aunt Natalie was mumbling, "Oh my God."

Uncle Karl was gurgling with sounds of the knife plunging into the center of Karl's chest.

Tomas was yelling repeatedly, "It will stop now; won't it old man?"

These were the sounds that replaced my screams. That was OK with me.

Now Tomas sat straddle across the bloody heap of Uncle Karl. He was heaving and gasping air into his lungs.

Then there was only the sound of Aunt Natalie. "Oh no! Dear heavens no." She mumbled.

"She knew!" I screamed at the top of my lungs.

Tomas stood to face her. He was dripping with the blood and flesh of our dearly departed Uncle.

"I know!" he said charging her.

"Tomas, no!" were the last words she would say.

Her last sounds would be the gurgling sound of the blood and air mixing in her lungs, trying, but failing to escape on the tail of unspoken words.

I would have never believed it had I been told of the carnage I saw that day. Nor could I believe that I would find some solace in this terrible scene. I would

not find peace, but there was solace in the fears, of the pair, that I no longer felt. There also was blood! Lots and lots of blood. There was so much blood that it was hard to believe that it had come from just these two. I knew I should be feeling anything but the relief I felt at that moment. I was ashamed I could not feel any shame for this scene or pity for its victims.

"It will stop now", Tomas said with a twisted, vacant look in his eyes. He said this with a strange finality to him. Then he dropped the knife, walked to the parlor and sat down in the old wing backed chair. The chair was Uncle Karl's favorite. It somehow seemed to be very fitting.

We three girls joined him in the parlor. I sat on his lap. Anna and Tereza sat at his feet. There was quiet and closeness among the four of us. More closeness than there had been since Uncle Karl first showed the monster that was him to Tomas and Tereza. More closeness than there had been among us since the poisons of this pair's evil had first stolen their innocence.

We were found sitting together, quietly smiling and gently rocking and touching each other. The postal agent saw us covered in blood through the window and of course, called the authorities. As they came into the room none of us even acknowledged the police and children's agents.

Tomas was sitting there smiling as they carried the three of us girls away. We would never see him again.

Chapter 7

At the girls' home where next we would live, we were informed Tomas was taken to the sanitarium. A few months later we attended a funeral service for him. We had been told he never really came back from that fateful day. Apparently he just sat in his chair rocking and smiling. He ate and drank very little. His health had rapidly deteriorated until he was found dead one evening.

I was now ten years old. Anna was thirteen and Tereza was sixteen. We were placed in a relatively small orphanage for girls just outside of Prague. Everything occurred on the facility. We went to school there. We ate, slept, and did our chores there. All supplies were brought to us.

There were twenty girls living there. All orphans. Also there was a priest, three nuns and a male caretaker.

I would listen to the other girls talk at the orphanage. I was one of the youngest. The things they discussed seemed very trivial to me. Emotionally, although I was broken, I had been forced to grow up pretty rapidly. I knew I could count on family and that was about all I was sure of. That, of course, did not

include any distant relatives. By family, I meant Anna and Tereza. Tereza had been very quiet with the other girls initially. She became very protective of Anna and myself. Anna and I were inseparable.

The three of us were what we had left, all we had left. We didn't trust much and after a few months counted ourselves very fortunate things were as good as they were. As for myself, I would lose myself in books. I was either in class with Anna, taking out the trash with Anna (our chore), swinging with Anna or reading with Anna while Tereza brushed our hair.

The other girls were a blend of orphan girls. All orphaned by some tragedy. All thrown away by society. We were a collection of humans swept under a rug, only to be mentioned in apologetic whispers by polite people of the towns and cities we once called our homes. They couldn't get involved or be bothered by us or rather the thought of us. They would donate or whatever it was they did so it no longer bothered them that nothing was done.

We never saw anyone; ever! There were some drugs, mostly pot and alcohol that some of the girls had and used. Sometimes they would have mushrooms, coke or less often heroin.

It was the older girls that had the drugs. I tried wine and pot a couple of times. On Saturday we got to watch some movies as long as the nuns did not deem it too racy. There was rumor the caretaker, Cerny, was the source of the drugs. Also, he did things with the girls; things like what Uncle Karl did. I watched him

leer at the older girls. He would watch them as they did their work. He was a pervert and I had very little contact with him. Anna and I both made sure we were never alone with him, even though he did not seem to pay much attention to us.

Tereza was a beautiful, hazel eyed brunette. I noticed that Cerny often watched her. She had really become curvy; meaning large breasted and full hipped. Many of the other girls seemed to like her too. Sometimes I would even notice she would come from a barn or a corner or a tree with one of the older girls. At the time I was sure they had been wrestling. I now know that she had found less threatening the pleasures of a woman's company.

Tereza was made to clean the priest's quarters. She was always more quiet than normal when she returned on Saturday mornings after she had been driven up the road to his home. She had become much more outgoing with time and her quietness, on those mornings, was much more noticeable because of it.

I would find out later that he had been a big fan of the philosophy that getting your cock sucked off was not "sexual relations", and that Tereza had been required to clean his pipes as well as his home. She had also begun to show up with more drugs and had been high a lot more these days. Anna had really begun to develop physically, and I noticed her spending more time with the other girls. I was beginning to hang out with a twelve-year-old girl named Katerina. We had been there a little longer than a year then.

I was now eleven and my body was changing very quickly. My breasts were now showing. They would become large and my hips widened. I was also getting taller and my waist was thinning. My lips were becoming full, and as if it were possible, my eyes were getting a much more penetrating green.

I knew what was happening and it was looking as though by fall, I was going to be the best looking young woman in a crowd of pretty attractive girls.

One evening not too much later as Katerina and I were giggling and listening to an American group, Duran Duran, on the cassette player, she kissed me. It was awkward and then I just went with it. I became wet down there. I was caught way off guard and pulled away. I smiled and giggled as I heard "My Name is Rio" in the background. I realized I liked what had just happened. It was the first time that it occurred to me this kind of touching could be fun. So began the next part of my education.

Chapter 8

There is some power in sex! As I was nearing my twelfth birthday, it was more and more apparent that everyone around me was doing it in some way or shape or form. The girls that Cerny was around the most had the most drugs and the more expensive varieties. Tereza would often speak to Anna and myself about some of the wonderful things she ate at the priest's house. I am now speaking of food, exotic and exquisite foods. She would speak of expensive red wines, filet mignon, beef cutlet, and caviar. Obviously these expensive treats were for sex of sorts. It was either for blow jobs or house cleaning. What do you think the good father deemed worthy of special treats? Anna was doing more and more drugs and she was, you guessed it, often seen around our creepy caretaker.

As for me, the times I was spending with Katerina were getting more and more fun. I was now twelve and not only was Katerina the recipient of my first kiss, but my first orgasm as well. We would get together and sneak off to smoke pot and drink vodka together. Then we would make out and listen to American cassette tapes. Artists like Prince, Journey, Air Supply, Bon Jovi, Poison, Motley Crue, REO

Speedwagon. We would get high, kiss and lick each other. We were each other's secret girlfriends, all except for the part about everyone knowing about it. I did not look to be twelve, more like seventeen. I was the hottest girl of all of us. All the girls wanted me, but I was in love with Katerina. It was puppy love, but love none the less.

I was also no longer the youngest girl here. There were, however, still about the same number of girls here. Every so often one of the older pretty girls would steal away in the night leaving all her things in search of a better life. We would always imagine these dreams had been discovered. We had discovered that sex was fun and also there could be rewards in it as well. There was power in sex and obviously these pretty girls had found ways to make this power work for them.

Katerina, my sexy fifteen-year-old girlfriend, and I would listen to our cassette tapes, get buzzed up, and make out. Then we would imagine the glamorous lives the girls who ran off were now living. These were not all that odd as far as dreams went. Most of the other girls also dreamed of another place for these girls we had known. Of course, this other place we created in these dreams was a wonderful place since we attached our futures to these fantasies as well. Little did we know, although sex is power, it does not always mean that just because it is your sex that you get to keep all the power. Another piece of my education right there. Lack of knowledge when you need it is

never a good thing. Oh and it will always be punished.
Always!

I would lay around high during my free time
with Katerina. We would dream of the luxury and
opulence that surely our old dorm mates were now
enjoying. The truth was I was pretty happy right here
and right now with my girl. These were good times.

Tereza had turned eighteen and moved into her
own quarters and was receiving a small salary.
Remember sex has power.

Anna was now Cerny's favorite. Katerina and I
were having fun. I was almost thirteen and I was going
on thirty. Not long ago, Katerina and I had done some
cocaine.

Anna and I saw very little of Tereza these days.
Anna was around less and less, but we still saw her at
school. Her free time kept her hid out much closer to
Cerny. Anyway, Katerina wanted to do some more
cocaine and mess around together. I decided to talk to
Anna about it. We made arrangements to meet up
Saturday afternoon out in the barn loft.

Anna showed up and said we were waiting to
meet Cerny. The three of us smoked a joint out there.
As we finished it up we heard a vehicle pull up. As we
saw Cerny's head crown the floor of the loft coming up
the ladder, we were grabbed from behind. I felt a cloth
filled hand cover my mouth before everything went
black.

Chapter 9

I awoke in what I was to find out was Belgrade. Anna, Katerina, and I were in a motel room of sorts. All except the able to leave part. The music was piped in and loud enough that we could just barely hear ourselves talking to each other. The door was locked from the outside and it and the walls were filthy.. The lighting was dim, and my head hurt and I was dizzy. The feeling I had in my stomach and the way my head felt left me pretty sure we had been drugged. Then I was certain by the voices heard when the door opened to provide us food, we were not in Czechoslovakia. The accents were different too. I had picked up that our captors were Nicolai and Sergi and they were now our guards. I had also found out they worked for Peter. After about two days, the two guards unlocked the door and stepped all the way into the room.

Nicolai said, "You, you, no not you, you two." Motioning for Anna and Katerina to go with him and Sergi.

"No!" I exclaimed lunging toward them.

I was backhanded for my trouble.

For the next twelve hours I lay there not knowing anything other than this sucks and it can't be good. Wherever we had gone, I was pretty sure we had found out where all of the girls who ran off ended up. How wonderful! We had found the orphan girl's paradise.

I lay there worried sick for Anna and Katerina. I also felt guilty since I was grateful I was not with them. I was pretty sure that as bad as this was for me, it was much worse for them. The thought crossed my mind that I might never see them again and maybe that I was up next.

About the time I really, really began to panic there was noise around the door. The door then opened up and two very doped up girls landed on the bed next to me. The door closed and then the TV came on. Anna and Katerina both smelled of sex and they were fucked up. The door opened again and a tray of food was placed on the dresser by the door. For a while, though, the three of us just lay there. I held the two of them and could tell there was more to this new terror than I knew.

After a little while they began to stir around a bit. We all nibbled at our food. The background music was still there, but now we had TV with captions. Even though we could not hear it, we could watch. The noise level was such we could talk to each other some. As we began to speak, it became obvious what had been a relatively pleasant period of my life was now over.

Looking back, it is really pitiful my existence at an orphanage was a pleasant period of my life. What I was hearing from Anna and Katerina wasn't pleasant at all. My role in our new life was less unpleasant, but unpleasant nonetheless. They had been taken downstairs and down the hall into a room almost like the one we were in. The only initial difference was split twin beds with black plastic sheeting separating them. The next difference was the frequency of guests. They had each been fucked about twenty times since they had left the room earlier. The men had been rough. Nicolai and Sergi had injected drugs into their veins. A cocktail of some sort. The men had not even been required to wear condoms. This was horrible!

A little while later we met Peter. Whereas Nicolai and Sergi were largish brutes, Peter was tall and lean. He reeked of money; exuding power and control. He was confident and even attractive. Then he opened his mouth. Prior to that, he had a charisma that made you instantly have a hopeful feeling or something like it. In reality, he was a very cruel man. He calmly but with force said, "This is your life now girls. I am your owner. I bought you and I will do with you as I please. I know where to find your sister, Tereza, and unless you want to hear about her grisly death, you will do as you are fucking told!!

"Nicolai, Sergi, these two work every day. This one is for the monthly auction. She will draw a very nice price. I know a couple of them will really like her. Do not sample the merchandise!" As he finished, he

slapped them both like testing the merchandise had been a problem before and then he left.

For the next two and a half weeks this was my life. I sat alone thinking about my fifteen-year-old sister and my fifteen-year-old girlfriend getting humped on and sweated on and came on and in. After that, each day I had the pleasure of trying to help them find whatever strength they could muster to try and piece themselves back together through the fog of the drugs and the haze of the physical pain. Last, but not least, I would try to heal whatever I could of the emotional pain left over from the act of smiling and being forced to politely greet and welcome your personal rapist twenty fucking times a day. At a couple of thousand a day, they were earning anywhere from twelve to fifteen thousand a week for Peter's little twisted empire.

When I was not trying to help them find some happiness, I thought about being auctioned off. I turned thirteen while waiting for my day at auction. By the ripe old age of thirteen I already hated change more than most folk and rightly so. I was becoming terrified of change. Each time things seemed to get worse. Now my love for my sister, Tereza, was what I worried about. I am not a stupid girl and the writing on the wall said I wouldn't have to worry about Anna and Katerina much longer. This is where they would die. Much of the time I wished I could die right here with them. At least it would end soon. I was sad, furious, and in a depressed state of hopelessness. No one cared at all

what happened to us. We were non-existent. We had
been forgotten. Think about it, everyone has some
normal, natural desire to have value to someone else.
The only value I had was the three orifices men could
fuck and all the pretty features that helped them get
their cocks hard so they could fuck them; that and what
could be charged to grant access to my body was my
value. I was so right about Cerny. To hell with his
creepy ass. To fucking hell with him!

Chapter 10

One day I was removed from the room by Nicolai and Sergi. I was drugged and when I awoke I was asleep in a very nice apartment. I was still clothed, alone and laying atop satin sheets on a large four post veiled bed. Through the veil, I could see a sitting area and off to one side a luxury bathroom. I simply closed my eyes in disbelief and went back to sleep.

When I awoke, I pinched myself and opened my eyes. I was still there in the quarters of a gilded princess atop a bed of satin sheets. I got up and checked the door. Locked! Dammit! Anyway at least it was clean and peaceful. I undressed and began to run a bath for myself. I decided to try and go with it for a moment or two. Hell, how bad could it be compared to what my life had already been. You know in retrospect I was often times pretty dumb for a smart girl.

There was a jar of bath salts and bottle of bubble bath on the edge of the bath tub with the shiny brass fixtures. The tub was deep and the water warm. The water at the orphanage was almost never warm with so many girls using it. The bubble bath smelled wonderful and the salts made the water feel so good. It had been weeks, but for a few minutes I truly relaxed.

Hell, I deeply relaxed. They both felt wonderful. I closed my eyes for a minute and bathed in it, remembering the American commercials with the slogan, Calgon, take me away. Moments later when my eyes opened there was a very stout, very pleasant looking woman standing over me and staring.

"Hello Petra. You are every bit as beautiful as they say. I am Kristanya and I am here to help you. Soak for a little while longer. Then dry off wrap yourself in a towel and come into the parlor area of the bed chamber."

This woman seemed too nice, kind of like Aunt Natalie had seemed. Hell, even diabolical Uncle Karl had had the nicest face ever. As I walked on into the parlor area, Kristanya once again began to speak. She explained to me that over the next few days it was her job to give me the overall makeover so that I would fetch the best possible price. She went on and on about how lucky I was to not be just a slave whore. I was to be given a pleasant life. I was one of the fortunate ones that would become the concubine of a wealthy and powerful man. In addition to all that, my cooperation would help ensure the best possible home for me.

I assume she must have meant the correlation between the two. My guess was that the other part of her job was to minimize the fact that I was a slave, so I would just play along in turn making my appearance more pleasant and welcoming.

She did her job well. I was going to cooperate. I was really, really, really going to cooperate. Yes, I

was and would remain a slave. She was right however, I was one of the lucky ones.

I thought about my first love, Katerina, and my sister, Anna. I contemplated their fate. It was unthinkable what they would endure before their death, a death that I believed would be coming quickly for them. There was no chance for any joy in between this time and that. I would help this woman the best I could. She was my best chance for any kind of life. Actually, she was my only chance.

I thought about escape and then thought better of it when Tereza crossed through my mind. My beloved older sister all grown up now with a just barely acceptable existence. She was truly one of the forgotten. I prayed for her. I thought about how much she had endured. How she must have wept when Uncle Karl first had her in his web, when he stole her innocence. The pain of mother and father's death still fresh in her heart and memory. How strong she and Tomas had been to endure him for Anna and me. I could only hope that I would someday have her strength. Now, today, I must honor her strength by having the strength to see where this road could lead. Anna was lost to us. Tomas was dead. Tereza had sacrificed her happiness for us and would be killed if I did not cooperate with my new owner's wishes. I owed it to my family's memory and to Tereza to do whatever I could to keep our flame alive.

That was difficult, but not impossible. Besides it was the closest thing to right I could do. It even

began to be kind of fun. I was lotioned up and perfumed. My face, feet and hands were exfoliated and moisturized. My hands and feet were pampered with the nicest, most luxurious methods known at the time. There were massages and mud treatments. I was measured by tailors and fitted for shoes. Hell folks, I was having a great time. This was more fun than a tea party. Whoa, a tea party. There was a nice dose of negative imagery. Somehow I knew that this is pretty much where this metaphorical tea party ends anyway. There was at least something a little less sinister about all this. Like I said, I went with it and even let myself enjoy it some.

I lounged around drinking fresh juices and having whole grain, fresh breads with fresh fruits. I was covered in fine robes and I watched TV without reading captions. For a few too many short days I was living the dream of fantasy the other girls and I had back at the orphanage. I was, as I mentioned, a gilded princess in a palace full of royals. Well, that is how it felt for me anyway. I was not going to hear any different. At least not until I absolutely had to. Wonderfully enough, Kristanya never again mentioned the auction. Until…

On the fourth day, Kristanya appeared with two young Asian women with cute bodies, but rather plain faces. They were carrying a makeup bag and a beautiful dress with matching Jimmy Choo shoes. My toes and fingers were done beautifully. A gay man entered and would cut my hair. He and Kristanya

selected a bob for my flame red hair. The dress was Emerald and sequined. The shoes were a shiny green color with about a three-inch heel. I was a knockout! Wow! I could not believe how gorgeous I looked. I understood how others had seen the potential for this much beauty in me now. I realized I was merely a product, but I was a great looking product for sure.

Kristanya sat me down as the Asian women walked out with the dress and shoes and began to button me up. She extolled my virtues and made sure I understood how beautiful I looked.

Then she said, "My dear, tomorrow is the sale. Tan today and rest. We will be in tomorrow to do your makeup and dress you. Good evening."

Then she walked out and I heard the door lock.

There it was, right where it always was, right in my face. Reality always is. Of course, we can always find deceptions and self lies to place between us and the truth of reality. Sometimes it is those truths that are necessary for us to continue on. Always though, reality will find us as if it never left. However, our perceptions of it, or lack of perception of it, is often times what makes life livable. Those who are always dedicated to the truth and only the truth, have not lived my life; would not understand. In that very moment right there, right then, reality slapped the dog shit out of me. I was always a slave girl, no more no less.

I was right now, however, determined to change my stars by being the most valuable slave girl in the

world. Tomorrow, I would at the ripe old age of thirteen learn how much of the world would operate. More deception and then even more deception. I would smile my brightest smile with all the fake exuberance and sexuality I could muster from the experience I had seeing women manipulate men using their womanhood on films and TV.

I, Petra Novakova would deceive others as well as myself, and my stars would change. I would use what God gave me the best way I could. I was going to move. I was a million-dollar prize. No one would be too cruel to something that cost so dearly. I was going to try to become priceless unlike all the unfortunate girls that were used until worthless. I would increase my worth. I would become a queen. I lay in the tanning bed for a little while and then watched television until I fell asleep.

I woke around noon and ate some food from the silver service that had been placed inside the door. Then I ran another luxurious bath complete with bubbles and salts. I got out and lotioned up my skin. Then I found something to watch on television. I did not have to wait long. My sales preparation crew arrived. Kristanya was obviously and pleasantly surprised at my wonderful mood and profitable attitude. Today was the real thing; not a dress rehearsal. In a few hours I would meet my new owners. Make up was applied and my hair was done.

Kristanya and I visited a bit as they were getting me ready to auction. She confided in me that she was a

freed slave girl and that Peter had once owned her and then freed her. She had not been as fortunate as me and had somehow endured and lived through the drugged out haze of this industries bottom tier. Something about her had caught Peter's eye and she had been prepping the prettiest girls ever since. She also confided that I was by far the prettiest girl she had ever worked on. I learned that it was only recently that she had been freed.

The warmth that had come from her was genuine. She did truly understand. I was warned that the threats made against my loved ones were very real, if I were to attempt to leave my next owner. A complete dossier on my loved ones' information would be turned over at the same time that payment for me was made. It was almost time. Kristyana hugged me and wished me luck. I thanked her for everything. I was most thankful for hope. If she was the exception, maybe I could be too.

The door opened and there were Nicolai and Sergi along with Peter. All three were dressed in tuxedos. All three were armed. Peter was nearly in awe.

"Kristanya, you are the best. You are absolutely the best. Wow!" he said.

I walked out with Peter. We were followed by Nicolai and Sergi. The four of us took an elevator to an absolutely plush hallway where I was taken to a velvet red room, locked in and instructed to walk out and strut my stuff when the panel that Peter pointed to opened.

Chapter 11

The anxious wait was probably about an hour, but seemed like forever. The door slid upward and I walked out into a well-lit circular room. I sashayed myself right out into the center of that room and plied my considerable young and fresh wares. I did a few spins and strut moves doing my best to imitate the runway models I had seen on TV. I could hear bids come in over a speaker, and I could also hear the auctioneer. The Police song 'Don't Stand So Close to Me' was also chiming in from its own speakers. Sting was singing "Young teacher, the subject of school girl fantasy".

The walls had a few cameras and I did everything I could to impress; subconsciously as well as consciously, I knew this was my only chance, my only hope.

"One hundred twenty-five thousand going once. No, I have one hundred seventy-five thousand. Two hundred fifty thousand going once, twice. Five hundred thousand going once, twice. My God, gentlemen, we have five hundred fifty thousand dollars. What? Six hundred thousand going once. Six hundred

fifty thousand dollars. That is right. We have seven hundred thousand dollars."

I did my best spin around coupled with a fantastically pouty come fuck me look.

"Seven hundred fifty thousand dollars going once, going twice, sold for seven hundred fifty thousand dollars to bidder number four."

Bidder number four was the one. Three quarters of one million dollars. Wow! I did not have long to bask in the glory, however. Another panel of the wall opened and there were Nicolai and Sergi along with their twin brothers or what could have been their brothers anyway.

"This way Petra, please." Nicolai said.

I realized his demeanor was much more nice than it had been. All four of the men commented they had never heard of seven hundred fifty thousand dollars before they escorted me down a hallway to an elevator. I was the star, the best ever. The elevator opened and there was a black Mercedes limousine in front of me. Of course there was a limousine, seven hundred fifty thousand dollars. I was worth it.

I stepped into the back after the door was opened for me. Once inside I poured a flute of the Dom Perignon that was chilled and opened inside. The smell and feel of the leather was incredible. Like I said, I was worth it. The door shut and then locked. I was a champagne drinking slave, but a slave none the

less. Fucking reality! Always fucking up a good dream; isn't it?

It was only about a twenty-minute drive there. There was the front door of a magnificent palace. It must have been a mile from the gate to the front door. The trees were giant and old. So was the palace. We were on the out skirts of Belgrade. Another sturdy middle aged woman met the car.

As the door opened she introduced herself. "I am Nicolette. Welcome Petra. Please come with me."

I grabbed the drivers hand as he reached to help me out and I then followed Nicolette up to the door.

It was a grand door and it swung open with a very polite gentleman named Dimitri attached.

He bowed and said, "Welcome Petra."

As I stepped inside I was floored at the images that filled my eyes. A real red carpet spilling off a grand staircase right at my feet. A giant chandelier that must have been fifteen feet wide was full of the shiniest, sparkling crystals I had ever seen. The floors were marble and walls were textured and gilded in what looked to be gold paint. I don't mean color of gold. I mean 24 carat gold. There were green pillars inside and out. The bannister rails were flame mahogany. As we walked the staircase I could begin to see the statues, busts, and paintings that were lining the walls of the second floor. We walked down a lengthy hall to a room that had a fireplace in a sitting area, a gorgeous bed, and a marble and brass bathroom that

was truly amazing. We sat in the parlor area and a servant came in to light the prepared wood in the fireplace.

Nicolette began, "Petra, your benefactor is Milosh Suabodova. He is an extremely wealthy and powerful man. A true multibillionaire is Mr. Suabodova. I do not believe you are sixteen yet. Are you?"

"No mam. I am but thirteen." I replied.

"Oh my my. That will not do. That will not do." She said as she walked to the door. "I will see you in the morning." She left my new quarters.

At first I was worried that I might not get to stay here. This place was magnificent. I was so hoping that I would be able to stay. I could even pretend to enjoy whatever it was I would be required to do. I did not want the fairy tale to end. Looking back, I am certain this was exactly what it was hoped I would think. It was as you would say spoken like a true slave girl. I now find it difficult to believe that I would have been so grateful, but looking at most of the first thirteen years this was a step up I did not want to miss out on. Without it I may very well not be here now telling this story. I most definitely was about to add skills to my skill set and tools to my tool box. That night sleep came quickly.

When I awoke in the morning I stepped to the window. There was a hedge maze and tennis courts. There was also a pool.

"Hello, good morning Petra." Nicolette was standing behind me. "It is lovely; isn't it? I am sorry, I didn't mean to startle you."

"Yes, it is lovely; isn't it? I did not hear the door being unlocked."

She smiled. "My dear there will be no more locks for you. You understand what is at stake for you. The locks will be no more."

How cool, I thought, no more locks. I was free except I couldn't leave and I had nowhere to go even if I did. But this was still an improvement. She explained to me that I would begin school and training the following morning and that Milosh, Mr. Suabodova would be out of town for a few months, but I would meet him when he returned.

Chapter 12

For most things, Nicolette was my teacher. The next few months were a blur of learning for me. Together Nicolette helped me tackle the histories, the philosophers, mathematics and Latin. She drilled me in science as well as tennis and etiquette. We went shopping and I learned about fashion. By the time Mr. Suabodova was to arrive, I would know how to use my utensils at a proper dinner. I could participate in a conversation about most things a basic but good education would have provided. Hell, I could even engage a little in politics. He would be here in a week and I would be dining with him.

The morning came for his arrival in Belgrade. Word was he was to come in from Tokyo by plane and arrive at the palace by noon. Nicolette made sure that I was dressed appropriately. She, I, and the rest of the staff gathered at the steps to the front door. After only a few moments wait, I could see a gorgeously expensive Rolls-Royce approaching. It was silver in color and had a shining exterior. I had seen no one use this car until now. The car pulled up and there was a truly beautiful face smiling out at me. The chauffer opened the door and stepped out. Mr. Milosh

Suabodova was built well and he made a truly striking figure. He was over six feet tall with powerful shoulders and large strong hands. His face and hair color were very much like your aging actor Robert Redford in his early years. He was a beautiful man.

He approached me as the entire staff said, "Hello Mr. Suabodova. Good morning Sir."

"Hello Petra," he said as he gazed seemingly through my clothes. "Hello everybody else. Thank you all. Do go back to your duties. Hello Nicolette. Please escort Petra to dinner later. Petra, I look forward to dinner with you."

I bet you want dessert, I thought. No more than he had been here, he could have me for dessert. He was gorgeous.

Looking back, I now understand that in some ways, emotionally, I was much older than my years much like my very developed body. Spiritually, much of me was dead, much more of me than should be. Emotionally there are parts of me that even now as an old lady, I realize never got the chance to develop. Nonetheless, I found that I nervously imagined the evening with this beautiful man. I wondered if I would please him, as I had no experience with a man other than that monster Uncle Karl. I was acting like a giddy school girl. Duh! I was a giddy school girl. Even though my treatment was luxurious, I should not have lost sight of how creepy things really were. Like I said, sometimes we must create these parallel places within ourselves to make our reality bearable. In my most

current parallel reality, and at that time of my life I quite literally was lusting for him. Part of it probably had something to do with fear of rejection and finding myself cast out into a world that I knew had very limited opportunities for me. Part of me truly wanted to please him to express gratitude due in no small part to the fact that I had forgotten that I was a slave at all. I had some strange fantasy of a love that the two of us would find. I would learn that manners and feelings are not the same thing.

It was six o'clock when Nicolette showed up in my chambers to help me out. She was very proper and reminded me to be the same way; to go in with the attitude I needed to get through a grown-up dinner party. Nicolette was very encouraging as always and she had enough confidence in me for both of us. She indicated it was time to go and we went.

I was taken to a part of the house I had not been in. The dining room was an enormous space complete with a giant fireplace and fire. The flickering of the flames was enchanting in the way it licked the high ceiling in the oversized wood paneled room. The table remarkably was only about seven feet across and three feet wide. It was a very powerful contrast that exuded wealth. This vast dining hall brought home the fact that I had seen so little of this place. What I had seen was overwhelming already. It was all encompassing and that made it difficult to compose myself.

Mr. Suabodova was seated by the fire as Nicolette said, "May I present Petra Novakova?"

She bowed and exited.

Mr. Suabodova stood and turned. "Join me?" He requested and offered simultaneously.

He extended his hand and I took it. He led me to one end of the table. He sat at the other end. As he sat down a raspberry vinaigrette wedge salad with honeyed croissant and a crab cake were served. We visited as if I had no choice but to be impressed with this man. I was very impressed, and he seemed to be very impressed with me as well. For the main course we had a lobster tail and small filet. For dessert it was terramizu. The conversation was light, but pleasant. After dessert he asked me to call him Milosh. He then informed me that he was glad to have me in Belgrade and he would be abroad for the next several months. I was instructed to continue with my studies, kissed on the hand, and dismissed after being thanked for a wonderful evening. I turned to see Milosh sit down by the fire once again. I would not see him again for months.

The thoughts that ran through my head were exhausting. The previous night had not been what I expected at all. Where was the sex? I was acting like a horny teenager. That morning I was dealing with what I am quite sure were very normal feelings of insecurity. Did he not find me appealing or what? Surely too much had been made of my beauty for that to be the case. Did I say something or do something wrong? I really had a desire to be wanted and to be valued.

Pretty normal, I guess. It was the circumstances that were strange.

The following morning, I awoke to Nicolette's smiling face. We were to go riding horses. This was another first for me, and it was awesome. The animals were beautiful and powerful. The riding was exhilarating. I found a freedom that I had not felt for some time, if ever.

We spent some time visiting on horseback. I found that I had done just fine with Milosh. I was told not to worry. Nicolette could see it on my face, I guess.

I was introduced to the stable maid and was told Nicolette would require me to ride with her once a week or so, and also, that the stable and certain section of the horses were available to me. I loved the freedom of riding.

Over the next several months I would find the back of a horse tremendously liberating. I had become a princess. I had changed my stars. With Nicolette as my taskmaster, I was becoming quite the young woman. I was training to be a modern Royal; wealth being the new nobility and all. Nicolette told me I was to be his Queen. Milosh had purchased a beautiful, celestial bride. Nicolette's job was to prepare me for that role. Milosh was a modern King. Young women had been offered in arranged marriages for eons. A thirteen or fourteen-year-old girl once was of marrying age.

Page 65

I was learning how to direct a household, play tennis and be an equestrian. The education I was receiving was as good as it gets. I was becoming well versed in all things that are required of a true lady. My benefactor, my betrothed had provided for his own arranged marriage.

He needed no alliance to achieve power or financial security. He was worth over seven billion dollars. He selected the most beautiful he had ever seen. Of course, that was me.

Chapter 13

It occurred to me that this had happened more than once. I mean how exactly do you get set up with people like Peter? Maybe it was just a onetime purchase? Milosh did have many homes. Maybe he had a Petra at every one? Or maybe I truly was the most beautiful girl in the world? Just maybe I was his queen in training, and if not; who cares? I had the full run of a two hundred room palace complete with stables, huge grounds, a pool, tennis courts, jewelry and servants. I had Nicolette who in some twisted way was a fabulous friend, taskmaster, mother, and mentor all in one. I was becoming brilliant, and I was free.

I settled in to a routine of learning, personal development and luxury. Affluence agreed with me, and even if I say so myself, I had become quite interesting and remarkable. Apparently Milosh thought so. He had begun to come home about once a month. He would spend two or three days just with me. There were dinners in the grand dining hall, lunches on the patio and long rides through our own personal forest. There were lavish shopping sprees and occasional helicopter rides to a yacht in the Mediterranean Sea for dinner and a boat ride. Even the boat had a pool and

staff. This beautiful man had all the wealth one could stand. I only wanted to get older faster so that the two of us could begin our lives together.

I was a beautiful, ripe fifteen-year-old girl. I was certain it was time for Milosh to declare me of age. I looked eighteen for sure. I was becoming distraught by the lack of action from my benefactor. I was horny as hell. I needed relief and did not know how to really achieve it by myself. Then one day Nicolette came to me with a small gym bag.

The last parts of my training were to begin. As I opened up the bag I smiled at her. Here was my "everything you needed to know about sex kit". There was equipment as well. Inside the bag were manuals, magazines, how to DVDs, lubricants, honey, caramel, dildos and vibrators. Nicolette merely smiled and backed out politely excusing herself. I was on my own for a while.

I most certainly was no expert where sex was concerned. I was no total dummy either. Where sex with men was concerned, my only experience was a horrific experience that culminated in the continued decimation of my family. Also, the next sexual relationship I was to engage in would be with Milosh. The coming interlude would be crucial for my continued status in his realm.

There were instructional manuals about clitoral stimulation, fellatio, different positions for intercourse, masturbation, sexual physiology, anatomy of sex, and sexual philosophy. There were also videos on all of

these topics as well. There were three sexual encounter story books and two pornographic magazines, along with one old Marilyn porn video about her unquenchable desire for sex.

Well I definitely got the message. I was to become an expert at sexual conduct and contact. I am pretty sure I was to become an expert at sexual misconduct as well. I assure you I intended to overachieve in this department. I was going to punctuate my intention to be queen of his kingdom. First I thought back to the only sexual pleasure I had known, my first love, Katerina. I remember those first clumsy attempts at sexual conquest back at the orphanage. I also remembered how fun they were. There was a kind of beauty in exploration and discovery. Nothing was as pleasurable as the naughtiness of innocence or at least inexperience. I felt as though my future lover had made all this as a gentle request. The truth was that I was enamored with a wealthy, polite, sexual predator who had instructed his assistant to ensure that I was in receipt of instruction. I could not see any of that then. In Milosh's defense, sicko or not, what he gave me was infinitely better than anything the world had given me so far. Also, even now looking back, I am grateful that I learned all I learned. This was human trafficking at its best, still sick and twisted. All that said, I was in my own fantasy world and it tasted good. I planned to eat it.

I spent hours in those first few days, and I spent an hour or so everyday going forward preparing

myself. In the process I got a surprise benefit. I learned how to please myself. I learned what my body wanted. I had orgasms, multiple orgasms!! I became very much in control of my own sexuality and aware of myself. I was free to cum. I was at least totally in control of this. It was an epiphany! I was amazingly enlightened by all this and empowered as well. I also developed a confidence about me that left me with an even more beautiful glow. Even Nicolette noticed. It was so obvious that she questioned me about possible sexual relations with other members of the staff. I laughed it off after I told her that she was off base. My only lover was to be Milosh or myself. The problem was; Milosh was nowhere to be found. I had not seen him in forever. When I asked, I was merely told that he had business abroad and would be home when he could, and that I should mind my studies. I was sick of my studies, I needed to have my man in me! I had to consummate this new love and complete the circle. I desperately needed to have the power, the opportunity to cement my place among all his nice things. This was my life, but I didn't feel like this was my life. It was like all my confidence was phony, but not all the time. Truth is, I was insecure.

I was sixteen and getting very, very anxious. Where was Milosh? Where was he? I grew not so strangely suspicious of whatever. I was chasing a dangling carrot that I wasn't even sure was dangling anymore. Now I know what it felt like to be trapped even with unlimited resources.

Nicolette came to my quarters after dinner one night to let me know Milosh would be in the following afternoon. I was elated and ecstatic. The moment of truth was here. Was I ready? More than! Bring him on. I was going to bend him to my will or straighten him to it. LOL!

Chapter 14

I could barely sleep and when I finally did it was brief. I decided to wear my equestrian attire and invite him to go for a ride in our forest upon his arrival. I was so excited and it felt good to feel this way. I was so hopeful and for so long and so often I had felt so little hope. I would have my chance to prove I was brilliant and it was today.

I hustled around and took a bubble bath. I shampooed and conditioned my hair, leaving it silky and luxurious. I did my finger and toe nails. I lotioned and perfumed my skin. I was ready and I informed Nicolette I would not be coming down to wait with the staff. I would be greeting him inside the house. She frowned, but what could she do really? She was the help. I was the future queen. I was actually planning a dramatic entrance down the grand staircase. I couldn't wait.

I sat in my quarters freshening my makeup and watching out the window for my Milosh's arrival. The thirty-minute wait after I was ready was a lifetime. Finally, there was the Rolls Royce Silver Ghost coming up the drive. I watched and waited for it to park. Then I made my move. My timing was incredible. As he

walked through the front door I was descending rapidly from the top of the staircase. He looked up and I could tell he was pleased with what he saw. As I hit the bottom of the staircase, I began to run into his arms.

"Milosh, I missed you!" I exclaimed as I threw my arms around his neck and kissed him. I knew I looked hot in my riding pants and high black boots, my thick shiny red hair pulled back in a ponytail.

"Oh, I missed you oh so very much. You look so handsome, darling. You must come riding with me." I demanded.

Nicolette started to say "Mr. Suabodova must be tired," but I cut her off as she said it.

"Please Milosh please. Come on."

"Oh, oh, ok then my dear sweet Petra, let me change first." He complied.

He was mine. I could see the lust in his eyes. Today was the day. He would find out if he was pleased with his creation. Now was my time.

"Oh, thank you, Milosh. I will meet you in the stables!" I said and hurried down to the stables to make my selection of horses.

For myself, I selected a mare that was in heat. Catalina was a big, bold red mare that was all force and raw energy. For Milosh, I had them saddle up his favorite horse to ride. Shenandoah was a giant palomino stallion, extremely fast, extremely ornery. This was a horse king for a king, my king. He would

be my king. It was ordained by God as far as I was concerned.

They were saddled and waiting along with me when he sauntered up to the holding coral. Just as I had hoped Catalina's condition had the big palomino feeling spirited and it was obvious. I positioned her so that her ass was facing Milosh and his mount; that way when I lifted myself to straddle my red mare my ass would be facing Milosh as well.

"Come on. I bet you can't keep up!" I said as I bolted away towards the forest trails.

"Hiah!" He exclaimed and his powerful steed took off after Catalina and myself both of our asses facing our prey.

Riding is erotic in and of itself and extremely liberating as well. I was going to liberate Milosh, that was for sure. It was only a moment before the men had joined us. I could see Shenandoah's nose stretching out, his eyes connecting to Catalina's. They were communicating. I could also see Milosh smiling at me. He had a cute, provocative smirk about him that I found irresistible. It was time!

I pulled up on the reins and ensured that there was a quick slowdown. I then forced myself to tumble from Catalina into some leaves under the massive oaks covering us above I even screamed for added effect.

"Milosh!" I exclaimed as I hit the pile of leaves.

He pulled up on the big stallion and the horse whinnied. The tandem turned around to see about us girls. Of course, we were fine.

"Petra, are you OK?" He questioned with great concern.

Out of breath, I answered, "Yes, yes I am just a little startled my dear."

He stammered, "Haven't you become quite the young lady? The horses seem to be worked up."

My response was, "I have become quite the young woman! Oh and the horses aren't the only ones worked up."

This was followed with a compassionate, passionate and insistent kiss. Our lips first ensured their connection and then our tongues began to get acquainted.

Our kissing was energetic and breathless. Our hands began to roam, to explore rather. We were just beginning an exploration of each other that would last much longer than that day. I had set out a curriculum and I had taught myself well. I teased him with my tongue. I made certain he was both pampered and treated roughly. For the next little while and the years to follow when he was fucking me, he was the only man left on Earth. He had no cares and no worries. He would always leave satisfied, always!

I found that not only was I good at it, but that I loved it as well. I had become very in touch with my own clitoris and my own orgasm. In our lust both of

our goals were satisfied by my prowess. I was a hungry and giving lover. Both predator and slave, wanton and aggressive, yet submissively approachable.

From that moment on I found that I could be whatever my lover needed, if only I would listen to the pulse inside the. I needed only to hear the primal and carnal sounds of their desire. Then I had only to be responsive to them and to ensure that they believed they were the only one left alive on Earth. All this was much easier than you might believe. On that day in the leaves, beneath the gigantic oaks, a sensually empowered Petra was born. She was a sexual predator in her own right. This new Petra left Milosh Suabodova spent and pleasantly broken, laying exhausted next to a gorgeous redheaded vixen. For a moment or two he was the slave and I was master.

Jackpot! That night we had lamb chops and mint jelly with truffles and a sort of cream sauce. Then I joined him in his quarters and again we let the horses run free. Once again, for a moment, I was master and he was slave. I asked myself whether that term "slave" would always enter my mind when I thought about us. I rushed this thought from my head and focused on the King's chambers.

What a regal room complete with two large turrets. His chambers were much larger than about ninety-eight percent of this globe's entire homes. The two of us spooned. Mission accomplished. Finally, I would have the love that I deserved to receive. My dreams took me places.

Chapter 15

After that night, Milosh did too! Lots of them and often. I wondered what he had been doing before, but all we seemed to do these days was play and play and fuck and play. This ushered in a truly tremendous period of my life. Parties, pasta salad, yachts, port cities, casinos and my first trip to the United States. We never seemed to stay in a hotel. No matter where we were, he owned something. Madrid, yacht, Greece, home, Miami, yacht and home. Anyway, you get the idea. The most lavish of things were ladled upon me. I did not complain. I was certain that we would marry someday soon and make little Miloshes. That's when a guy was serious, when you were really in, children.

I was partying the globe with the rich and famous and I loved it. Who wouldn't? Let me tell you nobody wouldn't, that's who. It was so fun that as an old woman, even now, I am glad that it happened. Even though I had it ripped from me with the atrocities I would see and experience I would not give that time back. It was awesome!

I was only at the Belgrade palace about one week a month without Milosh, which was almost the opposite of times past. One of Milosh's Slavic

associates was Andrei. I actually saw him fairly often these days. He was wealthy too. He had homes, yachts, planes and helicopters as well. One day when I was in the stalls, I heard someone call my name from outside. I stepped out and was surprised to see Andrei standing there.

"Hello Petra," he said as I came into view.

"Cautiously I said, "Hello Andrei" in my best, I don't think this is weird, voice.

"I just stopped by to see Milosh and when they told me he was not at home, I thought I would come say hello and see what you were into all by yourself."

OK I thought to myself this is bullshit, absolute bullshit. Ours was not the type of crowd that showed up uninvited. Also he and Milosh were close enough acquaintances that he most definitely knew that Milosh would not be here. I was totally on guard. This was out of place. Something was definitely wrong. The only question was how wrong.

"I heard you like to ride", he said motioning towards the horses. "I hear you are quite good at it." He said fishing, baiting me, hoping that I would bite and I'm sure of other things.

This was as bad as it gets. He wanted to fuck! Oh, fuck, not good. I was afraid no matter how I played my hand I must lose.

"Is it true?" he questioned as he approached me. "That you like a spirited ride I mean?" He continued, still approaching.

He thrust himself at me forcing his lips on mine. Grabbing me by the arms, he said, "I want you to throw some of that tight pussy at me!"

He pulled me back toward him and placed his mouth upon mine.

I bit him on his lip. "Fuck off, you Bastard!" I yelled striking him with my riding crop. "Leave now."

"You'll be sorry Bitch. You should have just given me that pussy. Just watch, Slut, you'll pay for this." He snarled at me.

Dammit this was bad, probably really bad. I walked to the house and of course several members of the staff saw me. You bet they saw with my clothes and hair mussed up from the incident with Andrei. I thought about how this must look with his blood on my lips. I wondered if anyone had seen him leave with a bloody lip.

How dare that man, that son of a bitch. How dare Milosh! It is one thing to kiss and tell. Another thing entirely to tell in a way that would leave another man felling entitled to my treats. Was that what happened? Or was Andrei just a sick and twisted man himself?

I had no idea what exactly Milosh and Andrei's business association was. Then the thought hit me or rather reality did. Wasn't Milosh sick and twisted too? Damn reality always there poking its head in where it always really belongs. But who wants it to? How would I play this hand? How indeed?

Milosh would not be home for a couple of days. That gave me time to think. I was nineteen now and quite accustomed to the life of a princess. I would not give in without a fight. Andrei had sworn that I would pay. Andrei was powerful. Very wealthy meant very powerful, and he was definitely very wealthy.

I was terrified. I didn't know if I should tell Milosh or not. I was not sure what Andrei had done after leaving. I was not sure how much power I had. After all, weren't Milosh and I a power couple? Well weren't we? As these questions ran through my mind, so did the answers. We weren't a couple were we? Not really. We weren't married. He had never even mentioned it. Thoughts of happily ever after had always run through my mind never from his mouth.

Andrei previously had had long term girlfriends, but not a wife. None of our friends ever discussed previous women. Had I had a totally false sense of security? Oh dear Lord, unless Milosh believed me as much as I hoped, I was screwed. It might not matter at all. But how I approached the situation would possibly mean everything to me.

I would use the power of the pussy. Pussy power, that was the answer. When we were together, naked and alone, Milosh was slave and I was master. I would fix this. Besides I had done nothing wrong; nothing at all wrong. Surely that mattered. I had myself worked into a lather. I was terrified. I loved my home. I did not want this to end. I loved Milosh. I cried myself to sleep.

Chapter 16

When I woke, I was no longer a princess! I was in an OK apartment by normal standards. However, it was a gigantic step down from the palace. What the fuck was going on here? Was this just a bad dream? I stepped to the door. It was locked. I began to beat on the door. There was no response. I beat some more. Still no response. I beat on the door until I had given up and then it opened surprising me.

Andrei, mother fucker. I couldn't believe my eyes. There he was standing in the doorway along with Sergi and Nicolai. Oh no!

The three men entered the room and I was swooped up and carried to bed. In seconds I was cuffed to the bed with both arms and gagged.

"You stupid, uppity, Bitch. You should have just shut the fuck up and taken this cock. You are going to take it now princess Petra. Whether you like it or not, you will take it."

Andrei was giving me the run down as he pulled his rather large cock from his trousers and ripped my clothes from me.

"See how big I am for you, dumb cunt? I am going to hurt you with this weapon of mine. Then these two fuckers are gonna fuck a seven hundred fifty-thousand-dollar piece of ass."

He paused and stroked his dick to its full length and thickness. It was fucking enormous. I was terrified as he approached me with it.

Nicolai and Sergi pulled my legs up to my cuffed hands and pinned me against my will on my back, pussy up.

The pain was excruciating as his giant dick head entered me. Then without pause he rammed it in until his balls slapped my ass cheeks. As he began to speak again I felt like my insides were going to break apart. I could barely hear his voice and then he wrenched my nipples between his fingers and thumb.

"Look at me you dumb, fucking, cunt. Look at me!"

He wanted to gloat and he wanted my attention to do it. He was going to enjoy this and he was going to make sure I did not. I looked up at him through tears of pain and disgust. He pulled his swollen shaft out of me and violently plunged it back into my guts. He smiled as I winced in pain.

"You see these stitches?"

I hadn't noticed until he said something.

"I let Milosh know how you bit me when I wouldn't give you my rod. He was furious. I bought you from him for your original sale price. Look at you

little slave girl all grown up now. I lost out on you way back when. I would have loved to wreck that baby pussy. No matter. This will do!"

He began to saw that thing into me smiling. There was no pleasure for me. He chuckled as I moaned in pain. He then continued to taunt as he punished my body. He punished with words as well.

"I tried to tell him his idea of creating a lady of you was not going to work. That stupid, rich fuck. Funny thing is, it did until you betrayed him by coming on to me."

He continued to punish me physically and verbally.

"You should have just hit your knees when I told you to. Now after me and the boys finish with you, I will sell you to Peter for two hundred fifty thousand dollars. After you are used up by the wealthy you will suffer the same fate that your girlfriend did. Ah what a future you have, Petra. Being fucked to death in the flop houses of Belgrade. If I do not do it first. I can afford to lose a half million. Then I pay Peter to give you an unmarked grave next to your beloved Katerina and Anna. I understand they are fresh. It took six years for them to die. They set a record just like you did with your high sale price. We have always done well with Cerny's girls from the orphanage."

I screamed into my gag as he quit speaking and began grunting while loudly pounding away at me. It

was taking a long time and I was in pain. Also I was going insane thinking about everything I had just heard.

"Take this whore!!" he grunted, pulled out of my pussy and taking forcefully and wickedly my ass.

I cried out in total agony, but only barely audible sound escaped my gag. This mother fucker had just taken everything from me. Literally everything! My love, my life, my body, my soul, all this pain just because I wouldn't fuck him. Now he ensured that I knew it was him who did this. Even that was not enough. I had to scream out in pain while he laughed at my cries. Finally, he pulled out and sprayed me with his seed. He was quickly replaced by Nicolai and followed by Sergi.

I was almost unaware of what was happening at that moment. There was not enough of me left to exist here on this earth anymore. I was descending into hell painfully oblivious to the place anymore. I was certain that very soon I would embrace death as it came to me. Until I felt a sharp sting across my face. I heard a voice in the distance from somewhere else. Then another sharp rap on the face and the voice was closer.

Oh no! What now you mother fucker, I thought, as I realized I was still right there with those rapists.

"Hey, Petra, you little bitch watch this!" Andrei laughed this out as he once again removed his huge dick and proceeded to relieve himself all over me. All three of them were laughing.

Oh my God! I tried to retreat within myself and could not. There was no way to mislead myself about my own reality now. It was too unreal to deny. If things are too good to be true, they usually aren't true. Odd though, when things are too bad to be true they usually are true. Later I would wonder why this is true. Right then I would continue to pray for death. Things got worse!

After I lay there in shame and despair for a few minutes listening to them laugh and gloat. I got to watch Peter come in the room and purchase me.

"Well hello Petra all grown up now, smoking hot. You remember the deal right? We wouldn't want anything to happen to Tereza. She is all the family you have left. No?" He smiled at me and continued this time speaking to the men. "See you later Andrei. You two get her ready and over to room three. We have several first day clients requesting her."

As he walked out, I screamed to myself, "Noooo". No, I couldn't take anymore! Several clients. A chuckling Nicolai and Sergei uncuffed me, drug me to the shower, cuffed me to the curtain rod and washed me off. My gag was removed. I had only been gagged at Andrei's request. I could scream. No one would hear other than the customers. If I irritated them enough, I would go to the slum houses where Katerina and Anna expired. If it continued Tereza would pay for my lack of cooperation. I was taken to room three.

I walked into the room and heard the door shut and lock. The room was very nice compared to the

flophouses. It was still a culture shock. I heard the lock at the door and the door opened.

I watched in horrified amazement as seven of Milosh's friends walked in and began to undress. No way! This isn't happening. Wake up, wake up I said to myself praying that this was all a nightmare. Two of them grabbed my arms and held me down for a minute until they realized I was not going to fight. There was no fight left in me. They would all have two turns each before it was through on this first day at the new job.

So this was what a demotion felt like. I had been such a fool. I was always a slave, never a princess. I would say it ought to be a crime to do this to someone, but it is. That did not matter, however.

There were wealthy, affluent men pumping on me. The thing is, they were even attractive men. Certainly they could have gotten women without all this. And what about sheer numbers here, seven filthy rich men.

They all had known all along about me. It was no secret. It was an experiment. I had been a fucking experiment of Milosh Suabodova. I had even been a successful one at that. It would be remarked among these wretched men that I had been proof there was no hope for my kind of an orphan, a common street urchin. Profitable? Sure, but beyond real redemption and now certainly so. As I plummeted emotionally and spiritually into the abyss, I would be forced to listen to the familiar voices which I now knew were not friends. They were sexual admirers. Twisted academics with a

dollar or two bet amongst them here and there on how I would turn out. In between those not so random thoughts and the squeak of the bed springs straining from the weight of myself and the seven fucking me or sitting on the edge of the bed waiting to do so.

In between I could hear, "I always thought you were so fucking hot", or "God, I always wanted to come on those tits." "You dirty bitch, you like it; don't you?" "I am going to blow up your hot ass." "Ooooo that tight little ass is hot."

This was absofuckinglutely surreal. I could not even begin to fully grasp that this was actually happening. Demoralization is nowhere near harsh enough a word to describe what was happening. How about dehumanization. I was an attractive pet, an animal. No, I was no pet. I was a beast of burden.

I would find out that these men each paid one hundred thousand dollars to fuck me twice. Peter, had made four hundred fifty grand off me on day one. Hell, in just the first half of it.

As each finished his second turn they would exit. Soon, but nowhere near soon enough, I was alone. Alone and drenched in sweat, soaked in semen, drool and snot. Alone, less than zero, once again praying for the blessing of death. Longing for death's sweet embrace. I was low, so very low. So low that even death would not come for me. Low and alone, spent and exhausted, dead inside, but forced to exist on.

I lay there for an hour or better before I was human enough once again to cry. When I did I was releasing it in heaving sobs, each sob stealing from me at the same rate that they healed me. I went to the bathtub and soaked. Twice I submerged my head to drown, but the first time instinct had my head above water gasping for air. The second I stayed longer and as I inhaled the first lung full of water, I was head out of the tub coughing up the water, gasping for air. I thought to myself if I won't let myself drown then I must want to live. I don't want to die!!!

Chapter 17

I was laying in the tub with my eyes closed when I heard, "Good girl".

I opened my eyes and there was Peter standing over me. He began to squirt some decent smelling bubble bath into my bath water. He turned on the hot water. I saw that he brought in several bath and body supplies.

"Petra, this doesn't have to be all bad. I am going to move you to a nice suite. You will take care of only one high end client every day. I will provide some good food and wine for you. You will not work on weekends. If you like pot and a little meth, I will provide them. Now open that mouth and show daddy how much you love him. You are one hot piece of ass. Show daddy Peter that you appreciate him."

I faked a good smile and took him into my talented mouth. I finished him off quickly and returned to my hot bath.

He sat there and gave me the whole low down. There would be no unprotected vaginal sex, bareback oral, but don't let them cum in my mouth. Always wash them first and always wash myself after. I was

going to learn to be a high end working whore. I was a slave again. Hell, I always was. New role to play, new cast and crew and another acting job. I wanted to live.

I was taken to my new suite. Not too bad at all. Really nice compared to the alternative that many of the girls in my situation had to live in. Nice big bed, pit group, big screen, stair stepper, luxury bath room with garden style whirlpool and a kitchenette. I would see how things worked out. Five times a week, something special for them was no big deal for me. I still had a chance for resurrection. I was still redeemable. I most assuredly did not want anything bad to happen to Tereza. I would also not dishonor the memory of Anna and Katerina. I would again rise from the ashes and wait for my time to come. I would not let the memory of my people die. I would not only live, but I would be totally alive again. I guess that is what I am doing in the telling of my story. I am ensuring that the forgotten do not stay that way.

I at least would live and just maybe, I would someday find what I wanted if I ever really figured out what that is. For now, I would eat well, exercise, take care of myself and see where that would lead me. I would still get to learn some things dealing with the high end customers and in the sack I would surely end up teaching some things too. As long as I stayed the same and the status quo didn't change I would not have to endure being used like what I recently had to endure.

For a little more than four years this new routine became my life. I watched my shows and

exercised my body using the stair stepper to keep my legs and ass superb. Peter came through on weekends most times and got his wick wet. He would leave me some killer buds from Amsterdam and some crystal meth from his new Mexican friends. They were hooked in with some cartel from near the American border with interests in both Europe and the United States. I liked the meth and it helped me feel horny more often for my clients. Hell, I even liked fucking some of them. All of them thought I liked fucking them.

Peter was making a ton of money with me. I had made him more money than any other girl he had owned. Over one million in the first couple days of the two possessions; over one million. At about one hundred thousand per month I guess over the last years he had made a hell of a lot more than that.

One thing I learned is that men seem to bore with even their finest and most fun toys. Peter had shifted his focus to drugs. Cocaine, heroin and methamphetamines were his new venture. He wanted to be involved in the Cartel expansions into Europe, especially the former Soviet bloc.

It was a new millennium and things were changing in Belgrade. His friend, Pablo Riverita had been given a free visit with me once on one of his trips to see Peter. He had a great time and at the age of twenty-three, I found myself property of Juan Pablo Riverita with a new address of Dallas, Texas.

My stay with Juan Pablo began with me being his hot ass gift from Europe. It was brief and nearly without remark. It came to an end after about six months when one night I failed to show as much enthusiasm as he thought I should. He was drunk as hell on Tequila. The next morning, I had an address in Oklahoma City and was working in a little whorehouse on the south side. There were three girls and we worked the streets bringing johns back to the house to rob or screw. I was a street prostitute now.

I was still the property of Juan Pablo and I still had Tereza's safety to think about. I turned a few tricks a day and brought a few Johns to their own, personal robberies. Shoot, most of them were looking for excitement and robbed or fucked they all got screwed; right? I did as I was told. I witnessed an incident when I was with Juan Pablo that left me with no doubt of his violent capabilities. I knew he knew Peter and that was the link to Tereza. I could take no chances with her.

The incident I am referring to was an event surrounding a guy that Riverita was certain was an informant. I watched them beat this man for an hour and he could not or would not give up the other rats. After all that, still unsatisfied, I watched as Mr. Riverita broke out an exacto knife and began to repeatedly cut this dude over and over again with the blades set about a quarter inch deep so as not to kill him quickly. He had his doctor type guy hook up the IV treatment and begin to administer solu-delta cortex

as an anti-shock treatment to prolong the pain. Four hours later and probably literally not figuratively, four thousand cuts later he sat there near death. He did die. The guy was innocent, and when that came out, Juan Pablo laughed it off. He also had a Brujo priest around nearly all the time. Brujo is kind of like voodoo and is very violent and bloody as far as religions go.

So, for a couple of years that was my new low life, still much better than the life a lot of property whore's lives. Hard to believe it can still get worse, but it can get much worse. Then I was sold to Javier.

Now at this point in my life I was pretty well broken. The meth had made me more manageable and I had resolved to be part of this life. To just play my role. I saw right away that Tereza was safe from Javier. This guy was out of his league here. Still it hadn't really crossed my mind that things could be any different. I didn't have the desire to be anything else anymore.

Then Big Fella showed up. There was something about the way Garrett reminded me that I had been trained to be a queen. I had been wonderfully educated, with and without ethics, and was still very good looking. I just didn't try anymore. The way he looked at me reminded me I was destined for something else. Fuck it! Anything else had to be an improvement. I owed it to myself to achieve and excel. I owed it to my sisters. I owed it to Tomas. I had to try.

So then the story of Jimmy Ringo and Big Fella crosses with mine and I sit in the extended stay trying to figure it all out. But confused or not I was free at last. Free from sexual predation. Free from the modern day slavery of women and children.

I absolutely had no idea how to approach this all and was quite overwhelmed. Overwhelmed, but not outmatched. As I sat in the lounger watching cars go by on the interstate, taking deep breaths in between deep pulls from a cigarette, I smiled when I thought about the fact that I was almost totally broken. But I had not been outmatched by life yet. I could count resilience among my virtues. When I thought longer about my toolbox I decided to make a mental list. Resilient, beautiful, sensual, intelligent, manipulative, educated, worldly, strong minded, sensible and I knew what men liked.

These were not bad qualities to have. I had a week to figure it out. I also had three and one half ounces of meth, and I had a good looking sports car too. Not yet out matched by life and feeling less overwhelmed by the minute. I prepared something to eat, took another hot bath and into the bed to sleep. That would be the first part of day two. Get one hundred percent rested up. I could make it. I would make it. After I was rested, I would.

Chapter 18

I woke up to the next evening of the rest of my life. I had some capital or I would have after I sold this dope. Fifty-two, sixteenth of one ounce sacks to sell and four to do. Cash and carry customers only a few hundred for expenses and clothing and I could reasonably expect to have about four thousand five hundred in a week or so. I could repeat with five ounces that I could buy for eight hundred each. That is eighty, one hundred dollar sacks. I would do eight or so and use about twelve hundred to switch rooms, pay for a couple weeks at a different place, then groceries and some more clothing. If I flipped again with seven ounces and again with nine zips and then a pound I should have first and last month's rent on a decent place, plenty of cute clothes, a nice laptop, and a cell phone.

All that and a couple ounces of dope and eight or nine thousand dollars would be nice as hell and a good place to work from.

I had transportation and knew where to get some shit. I could use Marco for that. I also had cash coming and I knew some girls to dump product to. This could work and I could figure out where to take

this as it developed. This was definitely doable. I gassed up the Camaro and went to peddle some dope.

Whatever Garrett and Jimmy were into, it must have had something to do with meth, 'cause this shit was on fucking fire'. Word quickly hit the street that I had the bomb dope. Before I knew it, I was sold out.

I wished I could buy some dope from Garrett, but that wasn't happening. I would have to see Marco. I had been selling some to the girls he knew. This sleezeball would require watching. He was involved in this whole human trafficking deal. I was checking into someplace else soon, so I set up a meeting and went to buy a gun.

I had seen a .32 caliber revolver at an apartment near downtown that was for sale. I knew how Marco felt about women in general, and he had already had a slice of me when my precious owner was alive. I did not trust him at all. I figured that a pistol might keep him honest. I needed to buy this dope and move to a new location in the morning. I was hoping this would go well tonight so Marco would not know where I was tomorrow. Like I said I couldn't trust him. The folks I knew wanted one hundred dollars for the pistol. That included one box of ammo. I paid it and went back to my room.

The meeting between us was still three hours out. While I waited, I quickly packed up except for one bag of bathroom type items so that it looked like I was staying. I took all the bags down to the car. I hurried over to the Value Place and got a one week deal on a

decent room with a useable kitchen and moved in. Now I had covered most of my bases. With a little luck I would be back in business tonight. I had forty-one hundred bucks, a full tank of gas, and a week paid on a different place to stay. I had acquired a small wardrobe and a gun. Things were looking up.

Marco was to arrive about seven o'clock. By six forty-five I was there with two clean pipes sitting in the lounge chair watching TV and waiting for him to arrive. I had a little rum and juice and a set of scales. The pistol was visible on the end table next to me. He was actually pretty punctual, that is really punctual as far as tweekers go. So when there was a knock at the door about seven I was pleased.

Marco's sorry ass sauntered in like he was already enjoying this more than he should be. I offered rum and pineapple juice and he accepted. I asked for a sample of his dope and he threw me a twenty piece. As I loaded it into a pipe, heated it up and let it begin to crack back he said, "So I hear you want to do business."

It was a statement more than a question. I nodded while I put the heat to the pipe and the pipe to my lips. I inhaled deeply and really felt it hit nicely and exhaled. It popped nice and right through the top of my head. He sat there grinning as I took two more hits and then passed it back. He hit it as I sat quietly letting the rush develop.

"Not bad. I need some weight," I said to him as he exhaled.

The mother fucker unzips his pants. I can't believe this is happening. For the first time in my life I can do something in response other than refuse and be punished. I was prepared to defend my freedom.

"Why don't you get your pretty fucking lips over here around my cock?"

It was more of a demand than a question. I pretended that he meant it as a question.

"Because I am not a whore anymore for one. Secondly, I don't like tiny little spaghetti dicks."

Predicting his next move, I was already grabbing for the revolver. The beginning of the end is now. The end of my slavery and that kind of treatment that is.

Marco was jumping up toward me zipping his pants. "Bitch, you'll pay for that!" he exclaimed as his body and mouth both came to a halt at the tip of my pistol barrel. "Whoa girlie! Easy there!" he exclaimed calmly as we both caught our breaths and began to calm down.

We both stood staring at each other.

Through our panting, I spoke. "Look mother fucker I'll pay how? The last guy I said no to said I would pay. He had me raped and then pissed on me. I was a slave girl and he was a powerful billionaire. You ain't a billionaire and I am a free woman. I am choosing to do business with you. Now can we, do business or not? But if you try to rape me I will kill

your ass, Marco. I am sorry I insulted you. It's a touchy subject. So what's up."

He stood there for a minute then stepped backwards and sat back down. We stared at each other for another minute. Then he spoke.

"What happened at the motel with Javier?"

I explained to Marco that Big Fella's pal, Jimmy Ringo had bet three thousand against me on a quick game of Russian Roulette/chicken. Javier took second turn. Jimmy Ringo took his turn and made it before Javier could call it off. Javier had blown his own head off playing a game he boastfully selected. Afterwards, Jimmy told me I was free. The explanation showed the rightful ownership of myself.

"That's why I am not a slave or a whore anymore!" "So do you want to sell five ozzies of that for four grand or what Marco? Now I am just a real smart bitch with no tolerance for men who want to own me. Oh, and I have a chunk of money." When I paused, I shrugged my shoulders as if to say, "Your move."

He smiled and said he would be back in a minute.

I told him to come back alone.

He did and in a few moments, I was the proud owner of five ounces of pretty good drugs and Marco had left. I was surprised how relieved I felt, which meant I had been a lot more afraid than I expected to

be. I was pleased with the choices I had made to prepare. I was shaken, but yet now more confident.

I packed my toiletries, scales, baggies, and rum and made my way to the car. I was nervous driving with this much shit. I guess I didn't notice before since I was as freaked out about all the other recent events. I just drove the speed limit and kept my fingers crossed. It was only a ten to fifteen-minute drive, but it seemed like an hour.

As I unpacked my toiletries, I began to run a bath, a very hot bath. As it ran and then cooled a bit, I weighed up my eighty packages, cleaned up my mess and loaded my pipe. I took several deep pulls on the dragon's tail and soon found myself ethereal and horny. I got in the bath and smoked a joint while I fingered my clit. As my own rapture overcame the drugs, I moaned loudly short of breath. The combination of the natural endorphins, the endocrine system, the two drugs and rum punch was heavenly. I could feel the stress of the past week fall away like the dying leaves of fall, leaving only the raw structure required for rebirth in the spring.

Chapter 19

Things had not really slowed down much for me since I determined that Garrett would be my unlikely savior. Since, I had determined that I still had something to live for, ME! I had not really given myself a chance to reflect on my current state of affairs. I had done the reflecting I needed to do on the past, dragging all of the spiritual pain and toxin from the past out into the light.

Poison of the soul cannot survive in the light. However, if it is not dragged out and inspected it will grow after it takes root to your heart and within one's mind. It can even fool you, convincing it has given you strength and power then letting you watch in disbelief as reality once again attempts to destroy. The contrast between our delusions and our true existence can shock us to death, but an accurate inventory of ourselves and our souls is priceless. The thing is once we have cleansed our inners selves of the moss and algae of self-loathing and despair of those momentary lapses of courage, we fail to reflect again for too long until we do not know or like ourselves yet again. Since I was newly cleansed as well as introduced to my new

liberated self, I really needed to choose my path and myself.

There was a great deal of healthy pride swelling within me. I was playing in and even winning within a man's world. I was making it, but I had to make sure that I did not become predatory like those who had used me; almost to the point of used up. As I purged myself I had to ensure that I didn't fill up all the little nooks and crannies of my world, inside and out, with anymore crap. Now don't get me wrong, I wasn't aspiring to be an angel, but I wasn't trying to become a devil either.

I let the steam and chemicals lift away the pains of this world and let the relief inspire me. I still was unsure what I would become. I did know that calling another "master" could not happen even if it did cost me my soul. I hoped that the price would not be so steep. I even prayed that would not be the case. I most assuredly would never be a pet or a beast of burden again. I would live free.

I made some calls, and although the quality of this was not as good, it was most definitely not bad either. I suppose a lot of it had to do with the first batch. I already had become some people's first call. Business was good and I couldn't help feeling like if I had had a plan it was coming together. I noticed some of the working girls here and there during the course of my day's travels, that seemed to be getting the short end of it all. I wished I could help them, but in many cases that was too risky. I did notice that a great many

of them in the worst conditions happened to be Marco's girls!

I made another deal with him and like before had things set up where I would be changing addresses immediately following the exchange. I did not trust him! That aside, the deal went smoothly. Afterwards I moved. We did a third deal, again with no problems. Quality was good, price was good, and Marco was well behaved. I almost started to soften up a little on him.

You know, I think he must have sensed this. Maybe his dumb ass had even planned it? I don't know, but he made his move. I had worked up to eleven K and was needing to buy a pound. He said I would have to come by his place to get it from him. I didn't think much about it. It was a bunch of dope and he had been pretty well behaved the last couple of times I dealt with him. So I went to his place.

As soon as I entered I knew it was a mistake. He was clothed in only a bathrobe and there was Latin music playing. He had the light dimmed and a few candles lit. I pretended not to notice what he was attempting. In hindsight, which I hear is twenty/twenty, I probably should have said something when I entered.

He allowed his robe to fall open. I still pretended not to notice. He leaned in to kiss me and I recoiled.

"Marco, dammit. I told you that I was not here to do this. I told you how I feel."

He responded with, "But I don't want a slut. I want you to be with me."

Oh, shit. This beaner thought he was in love with me. Maybe not tonight, but this pretty much had to end badly and probably soon.

I went back to the speech about being a newly freed slave girl and all. I tried to keep the focus on the meth deal. It worked and I was out the door with a pound. I had a problem coming sometime soon. I knew these guys did not believe women were their equals. I knew that his ego would force some kind of problem sometime in the very near future. If not, these other mother fuckers would hit the juice button.

I made a mental note to check out my alternatives. Maybe I could avoid this coming darkness. I had seen plenty of the proverbial darkness before. I had seen more than my share. I knew there would be more sometime. Hopefully, just not right now!

Chapter 20

I found a different route for the next pound and got an apartment in Moore. I was financially secure at the moment and had twenty ounces of dope. Things were looking up and fortunately I hadn't had to think about a scorned Marco for a week or so.

I purchased some Pyrex cookware as well as some other products for the new apartment. Afterwards I stopped by the nutrition store and got five ounces of crystallized vitamin B. The quality of the shit I was working with was pretty decent and I decided to use a cutting trick I had heard about to turn all this into twenty-five ounces. I knew I could get a kilo for about twenty-two and if this worked out I could use it to make a kilo, forty-four ounces. I could easily flip that into twenty-five and an apartment full of furniture.

I knew this would compromise quality, but most of my customers were not the most observant creatures and I felt like I could pull this double flip before anyone said a word if I made it up with great service, something not real prevalent among most of my competitors. It was a bit of a gamble, but I felt as if I could make it work and it was worth the risk.

I melted up all the shit and dropped in the cut. Then I stirred and placed in the freezer to give it all the feathering and fractures that you want the shit to have. When I pulled it out of the freezer, I was surprised, it looked like money to me. It was the beautiful slightly cloudy fractured shards that kept them coming back for more.

What was better was all my customers loved it. I mean they really fucking loved it. I have always thought that looks could be deceiving. I have always heard that location is everything where business is concerned. Well, this shit was awesome looking and do-able. I made sure that my location was always right up the interstate and on my way to them! I was already half-way to the twenty-two I needed to do this. Then I saw Ciara!

I had stopped by to see Andrea, a girl that I knew, when I saw her. She was a little blond with a piercingly sexual pair of sapphire eyes. She had perky, small breasts and an angelic face. This girl was gorgeous from her head all the way down to her beautiful feet. She was sitting on the couch watching a movie with her feet pulled up underneath her. I just wanted to eat her up. Ciara, Andrea, and I were getting high when Andrea offered some juice. I accepted. Ciara got up to get it and I could not help but watch her move. She moved with the elegant ease of a gazelle. I nodded to Andrea questioningly and was pleased when she indicated that Ciara wasn't attached to anyone. I hoped she would be leaving with me.

I had not had these feelings or urges for a woman for some time. I had already determined within seconds that I was willing to run with these urges I was experiencing towards Ciara. I had already noticed that the feelings I experienced towards men were skewed by my total confusion where men were concerned. I would see something that physically attracted me to a man and then be repulsed by all the years of various abuses from them. The opposition I felt within my own feelings about men made the urges and attraction towards Ciara very liberating. It was very similar to the liberation I felt through all those preteen, anxious, safe and fun, bumblings with Katerina.

As Katerina once again crossed my mind, I sat on the couch and began to mourn and then thought better of it. There was the potential of emotionally safe fun in Ciara. I would embrace that instead. I caught her checking me out too. Excited is how it made me feel. Before it turned to insecurity or whatever else could derail this opportunity. I asked her if she wanted to run over to IHOP with me. She smiled and that was that. She nodded, got up and put on some shoes to leave.

We smoked a pinner of some good weed she had on the way to the restaurant. The grass was pungent and sweet. It helped our appetites while lightening our mood. She ordered blueberry stuffed French toast and I had an egg white omelet with pineapple and cream cheese. We sipped coffee and had light conversation. We were definitely hot for each

other. That became delightfully obvious to us both before the first cups of coffee were drained.

After we had eaten we continued to chat and the conversation turned a little darker and much heavier. She had just recently stopped working for Marco, without his knowledge. She didn't really have anywhere more permanent to stay. She had been over at Andrea's for a few days and felt like she was wearing out her welcome. She had heard a little about me from Marco. Something about an accident at the motel with his friend, and that I was a bitch.

I offered to let her stay with me for a couple of days and she accepted. We wrapped it up at the IHOP. I paid, left a tip and went back to Andrea's. We rolled another bowl at Andrea's and the three of us talked for a minute. As Ciara expected, Andrea was glad to be rid of her, not that she had regretted helping. She was just ready to have her privacy back. The mood was light with an air of relief in it when the phone rang. Andrea answered.

It was Marco and he was hassling her about something. I wondered what as she was talking with him. It probably wasn't any of my business, but human curiosity and the fact that I was finding my business and Marco's overlapped quite a bit these days had me wondering. She hung up and turned to me. "Get her out of here. Marco is coming over here and he is pissed off. He heard Ciara has been staying here. Even though I told him she wasn't here, he is coming. You guys go on now!"

We said OK and quickly left her to deal with him. I was not sure what her and his relationship was. I figured I would be finding out soon enough. We hurried down to the car and tossed her two bags in before we sped off.

As we drove back to my apartment I found it difficult to keep my eyes on the road. This girl was fine, as fine as they come. She definitely had my attention. I found out the feeling was mutual when she reached over the console and began to caress my inner thigh and rub the mound of my ever warming pussy. At a stop light right off the interstate she reached over and gave me a kiss.

I had not been this excited in a long time. The pink kitty playhouse was flooding. My face blushed red and her giggling face, pink cheeks and puckering lips let me know that she noticed and she felt the same way. We could not wait. As I pulled into the apartment complex I noticed her erect nipples. She noticed that I noticed. We were nearly sprinting to the door.

Chapter 21

The door flung open and we burst into my empty space. I pushed the sexy blond against the wall and pressed my lips against hers. It was exquisitely hot. That heat was insistent. As our mouths opened slightly, it became a driving force of its own. Our tongues touched and after they gently explored each other for what was nowhere near too long, we both sighed into each other. We fell onto the vacant living area carpet and began to peel away each other's clothes.

Our hands began to explore each other's bodies. I loved the feel of her little tits and her pointy, puffy nipples. I could tell by her forceful squeezes that she was enjoying the feel of my large breasts as well. I loved it as she caressed and probed.

Our mouths danced with each other's in nearly breathless harmony until her mouth moved to my tits. Her tongue hit my nipple and I gasped and began to moan as the first orgasm washed over me. She kissed and sucked all over my torso. I felt so very appreciated that she took the time needed to know all of me physically. She responded to my moans and

movements. She was the most responsive lover I had yet known.

When she found the honey hole below my abdomen, she did not disappoint. Not at all! She was alternatively rough and gentle as she coaxed my second orgasm out of the depths I was not even aware I had. I had heard about, but never experienced an Earth Shattering Orgasm personally until then. I was spent and joyfully weeping softly when she was done with me.

I had experienced, to some degree, sexual healing and was eager to return the favor. I was as attentive as I could be, determined to give as good as I got. I was awkward for only a moment. I had had plenty of practice with sex, albeit with men primarily. Either way, sex was to some degree sex and being attentive and responsive were keys to great sex. That and hunger, and was I ever hungry for this woman? She responded in turn and we lay there smirking and giggling with and at each other singularly and at us collectively. We showered gentle kisses upon each other and found some needed peace and comfort within the aftermath of our pleasure.

I learned that she had needed to pay off some legal fees not too very long ago and had gone to Marco for help. She felt like she just should have gone to jail instead. He put her to work. Now she was aware that this how it would be working when she went to him for help. What she didn't get was the split. He would charge one hundred fifty dollars for one hour of her

time. He would only give her thirty dollars! That's not the really bad part. The really bad part is he only applied ten dollars towards her debt and took one hundred ten dollars as his management fees. On top of all that he charged her two hundred a week interest on her two-thousand-dollar debt.

Oh my God! She had to do twenty gigs per week just to stay even and make six hundred in pocket money. Then he sold them their dope and charged them for their own rooms. I knew Marco was a piece of shit, but this was just fucked up. She wept as she told this story of selling herself hundreds of times and still owing fifteen hundred bucks. She did not check in and hid from him. She knew he would come. So did I. I would welcome it.

Ciara told me she knew about six or seven girls that Marco did the same way. I started to think about that and I had an idea. What if those girls and I started a service for men where the girls actually made something for themselves? I ran the idea by Ciara and she said she would help, but did not want to hook anymore. She also said that the other girls were hookers before Marco and that they might like it. I called Andrea.

I asked Andrea if she would be interested in helping me with the new project. Her only concerns were about Marco. She didn't hook, but she would help any other way she could. I asked her and Ciara to help with getting me a meeting with the girls they thought would be interested. They agreed.

I was sitting there thinking in bed. The two of us had moved into the bedroom and were sitting there watching TV. I liked having her in my bedroom. We would be there a lot, when at home, since it was currently the only room I had gotten around to furnishing. For that I was glad, since I very much liked having her in my bed as well. While smoking a cigarette I was thinking that if ten girls each did a two-hour massage for one hundred dollars twice a day and I kept seventy-five dollars each time. That would be around thirty thousand dollars a month and they could make whatever other arrangements they could during the outcall massage service and keep all their tips. They should all make three hundred-fifty to five hundred per day. I would offer transportation, booking and client screening. They would have a chance to get two days off. But, of course, could work extra days. I would need an office helper and five drivers for ten girls.

I could pay the drivers about twenty-five hundred dollars per month salary, and I could still have about $17,500 for salaries and expenses. I figure I could move some dope through the girls and offer Ciara a job as an office assistant. If I paid her thirty-five hundred per month that would leave me fourteen thousand for vehicles, wear and tear, fuel, and office expense.

I smiled at Ciara, gave her a big kiss, and we went out to make some money. We would need it. I called Marco and told him I would need to fly a bird in

forty-eight hours. He said that was no problem and I made him agree to come alone to a room I would be in. We agreed I would call him with a location in about forty-four hours.

Ciara and I hit the streets hard. I found her a little .380 and we both got tazers. We also moved a bunch of dope. Things were, with a little luck, going just as planned. We were twenty-four hours out from our meeting with Marco. I already had twenty-two thousand bucks. We had a meeting in the morning at Andrea's with a bunch of girls. I still had four ounces of dope left and I had a hot chick in my bed. Some girls have all the luck! I sure as hell deserved it.

After a little bit of sleep the two of us got around showered and cruised on over to Andrea's. There were twelve girls in the living room. I brought some kolaches and coffee. I laid out my plan for a massage service for upscale men. Everyone loved it! I was a hit with this plan and these girls would be able to keep some of what they earned, finally! I let them know that either myself, Andrea, or Ciara would be in contact with them in about two weeks. In the meantime, if they needed anything they were to contact us.

I found out also that it would cost fifteen thousand dollars to buy off the nine girl's loans owed to Marco. The other three girls owed nothing, but worked for low rent pimps like Marco. I had let all the girls know they should look for new and better addresses.

After the meeting I took my new girlfriend, Ciara, to get a chicken salad at Chili's. Then we went over to the apartment, picked up our pistols and tazers. We made a couple of stops on our way over to the Days Inn on I-35 and 82nd street to get ready for the meeting. We had packed a very small bag and we got our plan laid out for his arrival. I had twenty-four thousand dollars. This was money for the kilo plus fifteen hundred dollars that Ciara owed him and a five hundred dollar thank you for your cooperation gift from me. I was hoping for a reasonable response from him. I was also planting the pistols and tazers around the room just in case. I was going to play the rest by ear.

Chapter 22

He arrived on time. We heard a car pull up and then a knock on the door. We took a deep breath and I opened it. He stepped in and sat down in a chair by the door. "I have been looking for you little lady." His Hispanic accent was condescending and angry. "Where you been? With this bitch?"

I came out with it! "What the fuck, Marco, what the fuck you prick? Do you want to do business or not?"

He answered, "Si, Senora, but this is fucked up!"

"Look, here is twenty-four thousand. That is twenty-two grand for the bird, fifteen hundred for Ciara and five hundred extra as appreciation for your time and trouble."

"OK, OK! Petra you are gonna have to quit popping up on my radar like this."

"I know, I know." I said in return as I signaled the weight was correct and put up my scales. He stood quietly and finished counting.

"Is good then? OK? See you around ladies" as he nodded suspiciously

As he left I could tell that there were going to be issues soon with Marco. He didn't like this, but Ciara was free. I asked her to stay with me on a permanent basis and she said yes. Odd how most of the time when things get less complex they are busy finding other ways to get all complicated. Now was no exception.

We packed and I had her carry the bag and wait for me to pull up to the door. I took some evasive moves to ensure we were not followed and in a few minutes we were home. I gave Ciara a quick kiss and said, "Watch this!"

I pulled out one ounce for us and then put the rest in my Pyrex pot and heated it up. When the dope was liquid I dropped in nine ounces of crystallized Vitamin B and stirred. Into the freezer it goes. Viola in just minutes out comes the bomb. She grinned and loaded a bowl for us as I weighed up the shit. I was done. Our little empire consisted of forty-four ounces of meth and seven hundred and thirty-two dollars.

I put the six hundred seventy-five dollars necessary to pay the rent in an envelope and gave Ciara the other fifty-seven dollars and the car keys. I asked her to go get us each a pack of smokes, grab some Chinese food and put the rest in the gas tank.

She said yes and left.

I sat down, lit a smoke and thought about things. It is always important to know your enemy and your battlefield. Just ask Tsung Tzu or Machiavelli. It

was time to consider both. The enemy was going to be most assuredly Marco. He was loosely affiliated with some of the Mexican gangs, but not connected. He could cooperate or be overcome. It was his choice. As long as I continued to be a good customer for the Mexicans, I would be left alone for now. Long term survival had to come from legitimizing my business.

The service for men massage company needed about twenty thousand dollars for vehicles and about ten thousand in initial rent and office equipment for startup. I would also need fifteen thousand to pay off Marco. That's forty-five thousand dollars. I could make forty-four grand off of the dope in two weeks. I would have to flip once more before I was ready. I could, however, kill two birds with one stone.

For forty-four thousand I could buy one kilo of dope, pay the fifteen thousand, and offer three thousand to Marco for the favor of allowing me to do this. If I were to pay two hundred dollars to each of five large men for security services the night I make the deal, I would have protection. Another thousand for bills and food, fuel, smokes, etc. and I would have another forty-four zips of ice for the masses.

I would have enough for a pound and a quarter of shit, twenty for vehicles, and another eight for startup fees. Hell, I could probably even get Ciara and myself a living room full of furniture in the process. Once again, with a little luck; right? I smiled to myself and at myself. I was getting a little stretched out here. This next phase would require more balls than brains.

Thank God I was a ballsy chick. I had completely drifted off to another place thinking about the twelve girls who would join me and Ciara hopefully in prosperity. I thought about the fun she and I were having right now and was hoping it would last.

Chapter 23

I was deep enough in the pleasant trance that I did not even hear Ciara come back into the apartment. I snapped out of it when through the haze I heard, "Petra! Hey, baby, you in there?"

It was Ciara kneeling in front of me. I smiled at her and pressed my hungry lips against hers. I was aggressive and yet still gentle in the way I took her. I laid her against the comforter with an extremely determined insistence that showed her she was necessary to me. This insistence also expressed to her how important her pleasure was to me. This time I was demanding in the way I coaxed her cries from her. After the first tidal wave of her passion crashed in the shore, I was still nurturing the release of her aftershocks. For another hour I begged wave after subtle wave from her. Then I lay belly to her back spooning with her in my embrace my lips whispering kisses into her neck.

Our sleep had been deep and long and it expressed the healing we found in each other's arms. When we finally woke all slobbery, with matted eyes and ratty hair, we were rested and all smiles. There were lots of messages on the phone, which meant

money, most likely plenty of it. We cut up some fruit and had it with yogurt and raw oats while I listened to the voice mails. There was several thousand dollars out there just waiting for me to pick it off the trees. There was also a very polite message from Marco thanking me for my professionalism and apologizing for his initial reaction.

As I was getting dressed I thought that it was really odd and uncharacteristic of Marco to have that attitude about things. Anyway, we left to go get paid and to hopefully look at some office spaces. On the way to our first stop, I ran into the grocery store and grabbed a circular with business spaces for rent and we were on our way.

As we went about our morning's business, I explained my plan to Ciara and smiled broadly with her approval. For the next week we made stops dropping off drugs, and stops looking at rentals. By the end of the week I was ready to have another meeting with the girls. I called Andrea and asked her to set things up.

I had found an office space and had also placed a thousand-dollar deposit with the leasing company as well as signing a six-month lease agreement. I had also put down deposits of eight hundred with the electric company and two hundred with the water company. I had studied and practiced art a little during my time as a guinea pig in Milosh's princess training experiment and was going to paint a subtle sign myself.

The space was awesome and I was going to show all the girls as well as unveil my plan for our little

company as soon as Andrea set up a meeting. I had come up with a comprehensive plan that gave everyone a chance to make it, even Marco, if he was cooperative. Who knows maybe his voice mail was honest.

The space was perfect. It was near the airport and the Meridian Avenue hotels. It was tucked away just barely off the main strip by the Marriot. There was a spacious reception area as well as a smallish locker room with shower and fifteen lockers. There were also three good sized offices and a large breakroom with kitchenette.

I would be putting a washer and dryer in the locker room. The girls were going to be living in the office at first. I would be putting four futons and a television in two of the largest offices where the girls could stay. They would each get a locker as well. The smaller office would become a conference room. The reception/entry room would house two desks for Ciara and myself. After purchasing a conference table, two desks, futons, televisions, copier, fax machine and computers, I would still be within my budget. I would even have enough to purchase fifteen massage tables and about forty warmup suits in assorted sizes 2 through 8. That is where our credibility would come from. We would only do outcall massage and would appear with limited cash looking like fitness girls with a modest amount of makeup on.

We would cater to an upscale clientele that expected to be upsold. A clientele that expected clean, cute, smiling girls that were glad to perform extra and

expected tips. All the tips would be theirs. I would provide an option to pay with credit card and to tip up front with the same card. All of our customers would be screened and all would be required to have a card on file for a deposit at the time the appointment was booked. If they tried to stiff us, they were billed double as a collection fee. We would actually be a legit company with horny therapists.

Of course all that depended on one more successful buy from Marco and a successful sell through after. At the moment business was good enough to expect that everything with the exception of Marco would go smoothly. He was the wildcard and he could not be trusted. I would not make the mistake of trusting him.

Chapter 24

Andrea had gotten all the girls together for a meeting and I was about five days away from being able to purchase another kilo from Marco. I called him and let him know that I would be looking to fly a bird in about five days on the way to Andrea's. Ciara was with me and this would be the first real test. Could I sell these girls today? I was asking for a lot. I would be asking them to move and to put their things in storage where needed. I was requiring that they tone down their appearances and temporarily walk away from their lives. I would also demand that there would be no IV drug use. That was non-negotiable! I wanted to help all these girls help themselves, but I would not tolerate IV drug use at all. None!

I knew this was much to ask. I also knew that I offered much as well. For those girls who owed Marco their slates would be clean. For all of them, they would begin with a simple and free work wardrobe, and a rent-free place to stay while they got on their feet. It would also be a free place to stay periodically when they needed to regroup or if they needed to work extra hours. It would provide a place to rest for a while. Also they would have a safe locker to use as a home

base. A place where a fresh start was available even if they needed a few trips from the starting blocks. Last, but certainly not least there was an opportunity for them to make between seven and fifteen thousand per month. So like I said I was giving a lot and asking a lot. The only problem that could not be worked out was shooting dope. One time and they were gone.

I walked in the door and there were fourteen girls other than Andrea looking at us as we walked in. The room went from noisy to quiet. All eyes were on us. As soon as I spoke all eyes were on me. For a second or so I got really nervous, then I began to speak. I was charmed that day as the words just flowed out of me and then flowed out some more. I said it exactly as it should have been said. When I was done, I asked that all who were serious follow me to the office and check it out. They all followed me. There were five vehicles that day and a total of seventeen women driving towards their futures.

For the first time many of them were feeling hope. For others it was the first time in a long time. As for me and Ciara we felt pride and excitement. It felt good to do something good. In a strange way it was all about some girls who had gotten by in life laying on their back, finally getting a chance to stand up.

When we got there, I was still a charmed saleswoman and the women who would be part of "A service for men" were completely under my spell. Either that or it was just a really good idea. Whichever

the case may have been on that fateful day, when I was done all were on board. We had a beginning.

I had Andrea and Ciara get with Marco's girls and give me a list of the names on his roster. Also they were informed that they should plan on meeting there at the office in ninety-six hours. Andrea agreed to be there to meet them.

Per my request, Andrea had put me in contact with Kris. Kris had a few friends that wanted to be drivers. Damian, Bailey, Jacob and Johnny all met with me, Kris, and Ciara at Cimarron Steak House for lunch the following day.

T-minus seventy-six hours and counting. They were thuggish types, but I had been told they were reliable and loyal if treated well. I made arrangements for all five to be my security team when meeting Marco. They had a couple of sawed off gauges and some other heat. They were also decent sized guys and that was good as well.

Kris, Jacob and Johnny would be full time drivers for SFM. Damian and Bailey would be part time. I made further arrangements to meet with Kris the next morning at Jimmy's Egg on North May Avenue. He and I had other things to discuss. That meeting went well. Later that day, Ciara and I would meet Andrea for an early dinner where I asked her to do some other research for me. T-minus forty-eight hours!

The next morning came and Ciara and I made love and then made breakfast before we ventured out to see some customers. The day was pretty much uneventful. We piddled and by the time we returned home we had forty-one thousand for Marco and our security. We had also picked out and paid for our living room. Everything was going to plan, but I was still horribly nervous about the next day's potential spectrum of events. Ciara sensed this and was there for me. I was her princess for the night. I let her nurture me. Tomorrow would be difficult. I would need to be as sharp and rested as I could be. T-minus twenty hours. Sleep came.

Chapter 25

I awoke on the day of my meeting with Marco feeling anxious. I was expecting the other shoe to drop and I felt like I was not ready for it. I barely ate any breakfast while I sat there receiving a shoulder rub from Ciara. Sensing my tenseness, she rolled a small joint and made me take a few puffs. It worked. I was more relaxed instantly. More relaxed but not too dumb. I knew she was upset with me because I insisted that she stay here and wait for the furniture to arrive while I went to meet Marco. Despite that she was being a rock for me. She did not understand that I wanted to appear more vulnerable and that I also thought her appearance might invite more rage from him considering the topic of conversation for the evening. I had a hunch as well as a plan.

I arrived at the Econo Inn on Martin Luther King and Reno Avenue. I got the hot tub suite and called Marco with the location and room number. I let him know the office would have an extra key for him under the name of Chuck E. Cheese. He laughed and sounded pleased. I had Kris get under the bed and the other four stay in the van.

Marco arrived to find me in a hot tub bubble bath. I was naked and soapy. I invited him to join me.

"Marco, I do not want us to be enemies. Come into the bath with me. I want to talk to you."

"Well, OK. It looks like you are coming to your senses." He responded as he took off his clothes and got into the tub with me.

"I know you are a powerful man. I cannot be an enemy of yours and live. I want to have a business as well and I want you to help me." I began to stroke his cock as I brushed my tits against his shoulder and arm. "I can be a good friend, Marco; a very good friend."

I straddled him and fucked his brains out. He came quickly. "What do you need from me other than this?" He motioned to the kilo of Ice laying on the bed.

I handed him the forty thousand dollars and the list of nine names and explained the deal to him. I also let him know that our business and our friendship could last as long as he would let it last.

"OK. Is good. I will call you soon then Chiquita."

I was surprised at the ease with which he seemed to be taking all this. After he was gone, I had Kris come out from under the bed. We waited about five minutes and I sent him to the van to wait. After another half hour had gone by, I walked out to the Camaro and jumped in with a kilo of dope.

I started the car and pulled out onto Reno headed East. I saw the green Monte Carlo pull out behind me. I knew what the drill was! The boost was on! I hit my left blinker and moved over into the left turn lane. I was right. The green Monte Carlo was definitely following me. I knew they would try and take me once they thought I was vulnerable. I hit my right blinker and moved over to the right lane. I was going to turn right after the bridge towards the pipe yard.

I made my turn and sure enough I was followed. There was a desolate little turn off up on the right. I hit my hazards and slowed the car to look like I was having problems and began to head right to the spot. As I came to a stop, I saw the lights pull in behind me. I was almost frantic. If I was wrong about nearly anything I was fucked.

As I predicted there was Marco and some goon. They took the sack and placed it in their car. They had not noticed the headlights behind them because they had been turned off. They did not hear the sound because my radio was hitting hard. I do not know if they heard any of the four twelve gauge blasts from behind them. They never turned around and now that they were dead I could not ask. I did not care!

I motioned for my boys in the white van to get back to the hotel. They left. I carefully reached into the open car and grabbed what was once my gym bag and was now mine again and drove away.

After taking the long way I pulled up, parked the car and went into the room to find my little scared thug army inside. I smiled at them and reminded them to make sure they scrapped the van the following morning. I also handed each of them four thousand dollars, thanked them, and told them to be at the office in three days at eight A.M. They thanked me and left. On the way out, Kris promised to call me in the morning after the van was crushed. I called Andrea and let her know that my suspicions were correct. I also let her know I was on my way.

When I arrived at Andrea's home there was a car I had never seen in the drive. I walked to the door and knocked. Andrea answered and welcomed me in. Her expression was that of uncertainty. I walked into the living room and saw an attractive, older, Hispanic man. She introduced him as Victor.

Over the last week, I had grown nearly certain that what had occurred was going to happen. I had given Kris alternative instructions about how this would go and a thousand bucks to go get an old van. I had also asked Andrea to find out who Marco purchased from and when she let me know, I let her know what I suspected, and that I would need a meeting with this man.

Chapter 26

I did not know what he knew about things at all. I did not, of course, know how he would take what I was about to say. To make my anxiety worse, I had no idea what to make of Andrea's facial expressions. They most assuredly did not offer anything to soothe my worries. Kindly, she did seem to notice that I was stressed out and brought us two glasses of ice and a bottle of Tennessee whiskey. I poured three fingers and gulped down half of it, spilling just a little bit of it and wiping it up with my finger. He was watching me as Andrea poured him a double and left the room.

I was sitting there nervously after lighting a cigarette when he said very matter of factly, "You have summoned me here; why?

I apologized and went into it all. I gave him the whole story from top to bottom, all of it up to the minute. Everything that had anything to do with Marco. I then offered him ten thousand dollars for any inconvenience. No strings attached. I then asked him to sell me one pound for the other ten and agreed to buy a kilo every two weeks for at least six months. In turn I asked his sanction and protection from the big

fish and promised that I could protect myself from the other fish.

After I finished speaking he finished his drink. He let the whiskey set in his mouth a moment then swallowed. The pause he then took before speaking must have been less than a minute but seemed to last forever. Then he spoke, "I will accept your gracious and respectful offer. Also, I would like to tell you that I admire your courage young lady. I have known Marco was a bad seed for a long time. I even have reason to believe that he had done some informing for the police. You have done me and many of my associates a great service and by accident solved a problem for us. Thank you Petra!"

He smiled at me, thanked Andrea for the hospitality and got up and left. Andrea had already let the girls in the office. When Victor left, both of our nights were over. She called the girls and told them we would be by in the morning not to leave or worry.

I was in shock all the way home to Ciara. I stumbled in the door and to bed. Sleep came very quickly. I awoke fully clothed the next morning in total awe of what had transpired. I could not help but smile. Ciara was not going to hold on any longer.

"What happened, dammit?" she demanded.

I kissed her deeply and smiled at her.

"What happened?" she demanded again smiling.

I told her we needed to get to Andrea's and began to rush her around. I had not noticed the new furniture the night before, but did so now. I commented that it indeed looked nice as we were walking out the door. I filled her in on the way to Andrea's. When we got there she and Andrea both went on and on in disbelief about the previous night's occurrences.

Victor had already been by with the dope. I handed Andrea fifty bucks for dollar breakfast biscuits and asked her to feed the girls at the office and then bring them to the apartment. Ciara and I went to cut the product and put it up before the girls showed up.

So, there I was, free a couple of months and I was sitting with a hot babe I could call mine. We had a really nice one-bedroom apartment that was partially furnished and sixty ounces of ice after pulling out a couple for us before the cut. We had leased office space and had a nice ass Z-28 to boot. All that and we seemed to have a little luck on our side as well.

When the girls and Andrea showed up they had all already heard. They were all still on board and looking forward to a new way of doing things. I explained the situation to them and before I knew it, we had sold thirty-six ounces for thirty-six thousand dollars. We had twenty-four left and some shopping to do. It was time to officially open "A Service for Men".

I had three of the girls with valid driver's licenses go with me and Ciara to a used car lot on N.W. thirty-ninth expressway where I bought five SUVs for

twenty-four thousand dollars. Four of them for about four grand each and a nice used Escalade for eight g's for Ciara. The guy at the lot agreed to let us leave the Camaro for a little while. So the five of us went to the furniture and bedding shop over off of Reno where I picked up two futon bunk beds for nine hundred. I got two nice desk and credenza sets for a thousand each. We arranged for delivery of those items and headed to the Best Electronics Store up the road.

When we got there I picked up two thirty-seven inch TVs with built in DVD players for five hundred a piece, two computers, a fax machine and a copier. After dropping three grand there, I took all the girls over and we spend one fifty each on them at the Ross store. After paying up front for fifteen massage tables and a used washer and dryer to be delivered, we dropped everyone off for the night and went back to get the Camaro. It was a big day, a very big day indeed.

After a good night's rest, we returned to the office to find a scene something like a high school slumber party. The girls were free and easy with each other. They seemed to be unworried. I'm sure for many this was a first. At least a first in a long time. Over the next two days the guys were introduced and the whole staff had shown themselves. A pleasant surprise was that the other twenty plus ounces of dope had sold and I had made another purchase from Victor. We stocked the kitchenette breakroom with a thousand dollars' worth of groceries and bought an ice machine.

We also surprised all of the girls with Visa gift cards
for two hundred each and brought in a bunch of towels.
After getting phone and satellite service we were really
ready for business. I didn't know and couldn't have
guessed where this would take me. I bought some
gloss black enamel paint and painted cursive letters on
the door "A Service for Men" and our phone number.
We were in business.

Since I was contractually bound with Victor to
be a drug dealer for at least a while and since the girls
had done such a good job distributing the ice, I decided
to combine the two. By lowering the price per ounce to
seven hundred each that left room for the girls to make
two hundred twenty-five a pop and the service to pick
up the seventy-five for delivery. This would boost
sales and legitimize our appearance while we all
continued to be drug dealers and escorts. The huge
difference was that now we actually got to make money
for ourselves as well.

Business took off like a rocket. I was optimistic
and still ended up amazed by what I saw and
experienced. Soon we were averaging two hundred
appointments a week. I had purchased two more used
SUVs and had made aesthetic as well as entertainment
and comfort upgrades to all of them. All five boys and
Andrea were employed full time as drivers. We had
eighteen girls (only six were still living at the office).
All of the girls looked good and healthy. We appeared
to be very legit with our warmups, tennis shoes and our
high end portable massage tables. I was paying the six

drivers twenty-five hundred each per month salary. Ciara was making five thousand per month. I was spending another four thousand per month on health insurance for the eight full time employees, supplementing my subcontractors that chose to purchase their own through our company, another four to six grand per month in utilities and expenses and I was operating a business with a thirty thousand dollars a month overhead. The kicker was that at two hundred appointments per week that was fifteen thousand per week or sixty thousand per month. A service for men was a hit. The business made a profit of about thirty thousand a month. Not too bad for a Czech slave girl! Not bad at all! The whipped cream was that the girls were averaging eight thousand per month in personal income. They were able to buy jewelry, nice clothes and some were taking night classes. Our little devils were beginning to look and feel like angels.

If that was the sundae, then the cherry was this. I was moving eight birds a month uncut. The quality was consistently great and my buy price had dropped so that I was making about forty-five thousand a month with the dope. I was not making any enemies. I was making all the right friends and I was making a shit load of money.

Our little business, "A Service for Men", had become our naughty little money making empire. It had been a little over a year since we had begun. None of us had been raped and no one had died. As ridiculous as that barometer was, these events had

become very common place at one time for all of the female employees at our company. One reality was being exchanged for another. It was a real treat to see that these women were becoming much like newly blossoming flowers all full of beauty and inspiring wonderment. Also, I had a legal bank account with a quarter of a million dollars in it and had six hundred thousand dollars in a safety deposit box. I had totally tricked the Camaro out. It was off the charts. I had picked up a nice used Mercedes 500 SEL and wore beautiful pant suits to work. Ciara and I both owned nice furs and her Escalade was tricked out. She was my girl and she didn't have to pay for anything. Consequently, she had fifty thousand in a bank account of her own.

There was no doubt that this had been a huge benefit to many. We had even condensed the futon rooms into one and turned the other into a fitness area for employees. Even our young security boys had used this opportunity to develop their bodies as well as their minds. They were all attending the community college and doing well with their grades. I still felt like I could do more. I gave Andrea a promotion and raise and hired another driver. I also lowered my price to six hundred and had those two take over that portion of my business.

I had gotten another price break and was moving ten kilos per month at this point. I wanted to share the wealth a little. I also asked more from them both. That included changing Ciara's hours so that she

could have more leisure time with me in the mornings.
I wanted to do other things, but I also wanted to enjoy
all this. I had finally been blessed and did not want to
let it all pass by without learning how to appreciate
things. I had once done nothing but learn how to run
an Empire and spend time appreciating things. I would
do it again.

Chapter 27

I at first enjoyed leisurely breakfasts and love making with Ciara in the morning. It was not long though before I noticed that she was becoming distant. She was not nasty or mean. There was no hostility from her, but when you begin to miss someone even as they are in the same room you are in, this is never good for a relationship. Ciara became more ambitious which was a treat to watch develop. She was now making nine thousand dollars per month and Andrea was making six grand. They were also picking up good money on the side with me and the dope.

Two years into this exercise and I had just over a million dollars in my safety deposit box and four hundred thousand in the bank. I was beautiful and a millionaire. What a ride it had been to get here, and what a good time I was having most of the time. Something was missing though. Something more was needed. Would it always be this way? Would I always need something more?

Even now as I look back I am not sure whether I can really answer those questions or not. I would also venture to guess that that very uncertainty lets me know that I indeed cannot answer those questions even now

aged fifty-five years. Speaking of uncertainty though, it was that which took Ciara, Andrea, and myself to the toga party tittie bar one night.

As we walked into the night club, we were immediately drawn to the drop dead gorgeous blonde bombshell that was on display center stage. She was hotter than hell and looked predatory in her movement. Of course, I am sure that was on purpose. I am also sure that she is as predatory as she looks. All of this is as it should be. The three of us were ready to have some drinks and look at some nice asses and titties. My juices were flowing because this girl had them both. I walked up to the stage and gave Candy, her name, a tip and forty dollars to give Ciara and Andrea each a lap dance. She kissed my cheek and indicated that she would be right over. Andrea had been kind enough to order drinks. There was my double crown and coke sitting waiting for me.

As the girls were getting their lap dances I noticed a few things. The first was that there was not very many hot girls in the place. Now Candy was smokin' hot, but most of the others were fives or sixes. The second was that for all the bright lights, mirrors and chrome, this place was just a hair above a dive. They did a good job of covering it up at first glance, but upon second or third looks it became obvious. Of course, I am certain that by then the booze and boobs should have you distracted. Third there was a wobbly young doe on stage who had lots of potential but was

so uncomfortable doing what she was doing right now. What an awkward young lady.

I walked up to her while she was once again about to fall over in her platform heels. She looked up all embarrassed.

I giggled and smiled and asked, "What's your name?"

"Amy Jo", she replied.

"What the hell are you doing here? You obviously aren't real experienced." I smiled as I asked.

She smiled back. "First night on the job; shows huh? Look I need the money lady."

I slipped her twenty bucks and my card. "If five grand a month is enough and you want to keep your clothes on call me at nine tomorrow morning."

I turned and walked into the lap dance area to find Andrea French kissing Ciara with two fingers stuffed into her pussy. Andrea had driven Ciara there and she would be driving her home. I left! God dammit!

Chapter 28

I really didn't find this all that surprising. As I had said before there was a distance developing between us. I didn't welcome this, but if it had to come, then I was glad to know it was here. I was not bitter. Hell I still liked them both and did not want anything other than prosperity. They would just have to have prosperity without me.

This was pretty simple actually. I wrote a note offering to sell them the business for one hundred twenty-five thousand and letting them know I would continue to supply them product at twenty-two thousand per kilo. Ciara could also have the apartment furnished. I left the note and then went to get a suite for the night at the Skirvin Plaza. The note also asked them to call me the next day and to let them know I would see them this week.

I got into my suite at the Skirvin Plaza and fell into the bathtub. After a long soak in the tub I collapsed into the big, soft, wonderful bed. I dreamed a series of dreams, none complete. They were flashes of scenes. The scenes were a room of masked women, a Rolls Royce, a dead body in a casket, Amy Jo, a huge stack of money. I couldn't really make sense of it all. I

also did not care. I woke up feeling confident. I felt good. Then the phone rang.

It was Amy Jo. She was interested in the job. She had a driver's license, but no car. I told her to take a cab. She agreed and said to give her an hour. I ordered breakfast for us both and waited.

I called a realtor and asked her to meet me at the hotel's lobby at eleven. I had missed a call from Ciara. I checked the voicemail. She left a message apologizing and letting me know she would accept my offer and looked forward to seeing me. I texted her that I would have my lawyer, Tom, draw up the papers. As I sat the phone down, there was a knock at the door.

I opened the door for a great looking guy from room service. He handed me the check and I signed with a healthy tip. He rolled the cart back out and as he was holding the door open to let himself and the cart out, I heard. "Mrs. Novakova?"

I looked up! "Amy Jo come in, come in."

She followed me over to the coffee table in the sitting area where the gentleman had placed the service. We sat down.

"Eat something, Dear." I instructed.

We both began to eat. There was honeyed croissants, bagels, cream cheese and melon salad. To drink we had gourmet coffee and fresh squeezed orange juice. The surrounding space was wonderful, full of old charm. There were the sounds of two women really

enjoying food. Why was she here was on both our minds, but she broke first.

"Why am I here Mrs. Novakova?" she asked.

I responded, "You need a job. It's Ms., and please call me Petra!"

She went on, "OK Petra, this just seems very strange to me. Obviously I need money since I was on stage half naked last night. Obviously I am not very good at what I was doing either. I have a little boy I am providing for and I am struggling to do it. Also, I think you are probably a lesbian and that's why I am here. Petra, you see I am not that way. I like guys. I am here hoping that this is legitimate and that I could really earn five thousand a month."

I started laughing. I liked this girl. "You're hired! I like boys and girls, but did not hire you for sex. As you may not have noticed I am quite attractive and do not need to pay for it. I have money and need a personal assistant. I am an independent business woman that is in transition and today we need to go find a nice condo, somewhere that has a gate. Are you ready to go? My Mercedes is here. Let's go pick up my Camaro before we meet the realtor,"

She looked at me, paused for a minute and said, "OK".

We left and I let her drive the Mercedes over to the apartment. Then I let her drive the Camaro back. I went in and grabbed a pile of my clothes. Clothes would be all I would take. Ciara could have the rest. It

had worked out for both of us and Andrea. As bankers would probably call it, it had been an equitable and pleasant endeavor. Ha, I already knew I wouldn't miss her much.

On the way back I thought that this Amy Jo gal would be exactly what the doctor ordered. A nice, platonic well paid friend. We could help each other. We got back in time for her to take my clothes up to my room, hang them up and get down to the lobby in time to be sitting there waiting when the realtor, Audra, arrived. I waved her over. We all made introductions and that was that. We left with Audra in her Lexus SUV.

I explained to her that I was looking for a nice three-bedroom condo with study/office and formal dining in a gated community. I let her know that I was looking for something in the quarter million-dollar range that I could write a check for and be in in less than a week.

Audra and Amy Jo were both pleasantly surprised by this. Audra also seemed sufficiently motivated and indicated that she had three properties available to view in my range. She made small talk on the way there and never even noticed that I was not part of the conversation.

She showed she was capable though when I saw the first condo. It was a lovely split level with an awesome loft office and master bedroom. It had a lovely little entrance garden and a back patio with a small yard. The high angular ceiling in the living area

with a rock fireplace was great. The kitchen and high ceiling dining was great also. I offered two hundred twenty-five thousand.

She called and I found out my offer was accepted. I could occupy the space in three days. Fantastic! This was just what I was looking for.

Audra took us back to the Skirvin and dropped us off. I stopped by the front desk to let them know the expected length of my stay. Then Amy Jo and I went up to my suite. When we got back upstairs we sat down.

"That place is great, Petra. You know how to live; don't you?" Amy Jo observed.

"Enough about that. Look Amy Jo you have a little boy; right? What's his name?"

"Yes. His name is Colton and he is four months old."

"OK. Wow! He is young. Anyway, look, I want you and Colton to move in with me into the Condo. Will you be my full time assistant? You will get the five grand plus medical and dental and I will hire a maid/nanny. I am about to begin a new business and I have money to spare. No strings attached. You work hard. You learn from a self-made woman and you get a real chance at some kind of real life. I am demanding. Don't worry. You'll earn your money. It will be a good chance for both of us to do something good."

"Look Petra, this sounds too good to be true. Also I live with my Mom and she likes to babysit Colton. I just don't know about all this. Everything is happening so fast."

I began to laugh at her out loud. Looking back, it may for a minute have even seemed obnoxious. "Amy Jo. For Christ's sake, girl. I am not asking you to marry me. Call your Mom and ask her if she wants to live rent free in a bad ass condo and make thirty thousand a year in cash to cook, clean and watch Colton. Hell, I'll even throw in a little Honda for you guys to use. Call her now. I am going to the little girl's room and then we can go shopping after you and your Mom agree."

I walked into the bedroom and was a little unsure about what I was doing. Somehow though, I had this really strange and positive feeling about how things were going to work out. I also had a feeling that this girl had some real tangible ability and that there was gold in them hills so to speak. I was not sure how, but I just felt like this was the right path.

I powdered my nose a little and smoked some speed. I was getting tired of the dope but the money was still nice and necessary. I didn't even want to look at the addiction yet. I remembered when I had once had the profound, and probably correct thought, that the only real chance for the future was to legitimize. Not to look legitimate, but to be legitimate.

I walked back into the living area and Amy Jo was smiling at me. "All right, you got us. I hope you know what you're getting into."

We both laughed. "Let's go shopping!" I said as I headed towards the door. Smiling, Amy Jo followed and we jumped in the Camaro. "What's your mother's name?"

"Cassie."

"Let's go get her and Colton."

She blushed and then said, "All right. I'll call and tell them we are coming."

I feel really good about what I am doing here and still feel like this is going to be a charmed deal for everyone. In hindsight I think part of me wanted to be an Aunt, a friend and a grandma to make up for my total lack of anything that resembled a family in two decades. As we pull up to the apartment, I know immediately that I don't even want to go in and see what's what inside. I mean to say that I really can't tell you what kind of dive this place was. Amy Jo called it the Courts and was making excuses for it as we pulled up. They had only lived there for about three months. Cassie had been recently divorced, was partially disabled, and had a hard time getting work. It reminded me of the low end places I had been forced to whore out of for Juan Pablo and Javier, before freedom finally found me. I went in anyway and saw almost nothing of real value. I introduced myself to Cassie

and Colton and probably too bluntly asked, "Ladies is there really anything you have to have in here?"

With tears forming in her eyes Cassie nodded no. Later I would find out that the few possessions they had with value, sentimental and otherwise, were in a storage unit.

I said, "Come on, pack up, we're leaving! We're going shopping today. Even if I am full of shit, you can't do worse than this. You're moving girls."

Amy Jo paused. Cassie did not! She wanted to believe and was quick to pack for them both. We dropped the keys off on the way out of the projects. They hoped they would never live there again and without spoiling the story I can tell you they do not.

We drove a few miles up the road to the Honda dealership off I-240 and I bought Cassie and Amy a used Accord to use. Amy Jo and I grabbed Colton and left Cassie to do the paperwork. We went to the furniture store off I-40 and spent thirty thousand dollars on some awesome furniture. An entire house full of it, including baby stuff for young Colton. I wrote a check, made arrangements for delivery, and then we were off to the Best Electronics Store for ten grand worth of TVs, stereo equipment, and lap tops.

We stop by the bank on the way to the suite and withdraw fifteen thousand from my safe deposit box. I have extra keys made for both of them. After we are in the suite with the baby I hand them both fifteen hundred each and let them go buy a girls second

favorite thing right behind diamonds, clothes. Excited for them, I watch them run out to shop for new things in their new car. This all made me happy.

Chapter 29

While they go to begin the repopulation of their lives with the small comforts and little necessities that a small amount of good fortune can purchase. I sit and think how silly all this is. I then laugh out loud when I think how crazy this must all have seemed to them. Their desperation made them take a leap of faith. Not so different than my own desperation to heal myself, and to work towards the completion of my evolution to finished product. Maybe this ability to help one another separates us from much of the rest of the animal kingdom.

Strange, though, that the same desperation could have so very easily created slaves of us all. The predators out there, the wolves in sheep's clothing. This extreme evil that emanates only from mankind. Is it not this as well that makes us so much more depraved than the animal world.

Is it not the heart of man? Not the physical muscle or inline pump that sustains life giving blood, but that part of the heart that connects to the soul or spirit; our very immortal soul and the level of dark or light that has won that age old battle for its immediate possession. That same piece of us that can elevate us

beyond the stars or send us and others as our victims into the deepest abyss.

I sit and think about this ability, this dichotomy that makes human life so much more valuable or disappointing than say the life of a cow or pig. I whimsically giggle at myself for breaking out all philosophical, but I feel the healing power of healing another. Aren't we powerful creatures in our ability to create as well as destroy? I find myself so very grateful at that moment that my life is not one that has been destroyed and grateful that I was able to again stop some destruction even if I was not pure. Shit, aren't we all. All that thought and emotion had me hungry. Tonight we would have steak, potatoes, asparagus and blueberry cobbler with vanilla ice cream. I ordered and waited.

The food showed up before the girls did and it was the same young, sexy thing that had brought breakfast. His name was Greg, and I would be inspecting him thoroughly soon. He gave me a phone number, and I gave him something to look forward to while he jacked off that night. A couple minutes after he left the room, the door opened and in walked two smiling women and a good looking, happy, little baby boy.

The three of us girls smiled, ate and took turns giving Colton little bites of ice cream and watching him smile. Amy Jo fed the little one his bottle and put him down. After some cobbler ala mode, the two of them showed me all the new outfits they came up with.

I listened to and watched Amy Jo tell Cassie about the condo and all the furniture we had purchased to go in it. I watched and enjoyed their excitement. I even caught myself getting excited about the future as well. I mentioned weed and broke out a good, plump joint. We had a good, old fashioned pot party for the girls; between left overs, weed, cobbler, and ice cream the three of us started to get to know each other.

I found out that until just a few months ago these two had lived in a pretty good neighborhood in the suburban town of Norman where the University of Oklahoma is. They were upper middle class. Cassie had remarried after Amy Jo's father had died. Her first husband had died of a major coronary episode when Amy Jo was only seven. She had met Kelly, and when Amy Jo was ten she had remarried. He was a pretty good provider and a decent step-father. Kelly was an investment broker. After about six years into the partnership, he also became pretty good at sticking his pecker into women other than Cassie. When she couldn't pretend it wasn't happening any longer, she filed for a divorce. What she didn't know was that he had gotten involved in some activity that the United States government and the Security Exchange Commission call insider trading. Well to make a long story short, a week after the divorce was granted the government seized the home that they lived in. The same home Kelly was supposed to pay for them to stay in. Also, his accounts, personal and professional, were

seized and he was arrested. It looked like he was going to be on an extended federally funded vacation.

They found out that I was a Czechoslovakian slave girl who had stumbled into freedom during a violent game of chance between two men who were heavily involved in the meth trade. They also learned that I was selling my massage service, that I was a millionaire, and that I was between fields. I was not sure what I would be doing next, but it would make money because I knew how to make money. I left out the part where I was moving ten kilos of ice a month. Before too much longer I would be leaving that part out of the story forever.

The two ladies had been horrified by the tales of my life. Go figure! I guess that is probably because the stories are horrific. Odd, how far away all that seems now. Odd, how I seem to continue the struggle to resolve that which seldom crosses my mind. Aren't we all seeking redemption, the little bit of salvation needed to navigate this world's horrors. Is any one of us immune from either?

Another thing we are not immune to is time and its constant movement forward. Speaking of time, as I lay in bed that night, it occurred to me that it was time to figure out what I was going to be doing with my time, business wise that is. I took a quick inventory of my skill set and resumed. Two things stood out. I was expert at peddling ass and peddling drugs. I thought about the other night at the strip club. I thought about the improvements I saw a need for. I thought I could

make a huge difference. If this didn't seem like the perfect blend of skill sets, creative thinking and available cash, I didn't know what else could be. I was going into the night club business.

Before going to sleep, I called Kris. I was going to need a different kind of assistant as well. Even though total legitimacy would come, right now there was still some dirty work to do. I offered him five grand a month. He said he would accept. I told him to come over in the morning and he agreed. I had a very long day and I blocked out my thoughts and went to sleep to the sound of two attractive, happy gals eating ice cream and watching TV in the other room. I, unlike some nights, had the luxury of looking very much forward to the coming day.

Chapter 30

The morning came splendidly. I had an east window and greeted the dawn with a purring stretch, like a smiling tigress. I sat up, then stood up and went to the bathroom. After what men sometimes call the three S's (shit, shower, shave), I felt as they say bright eyed and bushy tailed.

I stepped into the main room and found two sleeping ladies, TV still on, mess on the table. I woke up Colton and marveled for a moment at his huge blue eyes, something I would do much more by the way. In those first few minutes with the little boy I was excited, something I now know babies can do for all grownups if we let them. For me this was my first experience with a young child and I was much more nervous than he was. I held him for about fifteen splendid moments and Cassie woke up, looked over at us and smiled. I smiled in return and handed the little angel to his Grandmother. I was Auntie Petra, awesome.

I ordered egg white omelets, waffles, coffee, juice, and sausage links for us all including Kris who should be along shortly. I had a big day ahead and I enjoy this quiet piece of it. While we wait for our food as well as our other guest and co-worker, I enjoy the

sounds of a grandmother feeding a grandson while I watch the news cast.

There is a knock at the door. I get up to answer it hoping this is Kris. As I walk to the door I think about how thuggish he used to act way back when. After a couple years in community college with steady work and a few benefits he had become a nice looking and acting young man. He had shed all his thugishness. We got along well and I knew what he was capable of and there was still work to be done. I knew I could trust Kris and was glad that he had agreed to come aboard with my next enterprise.

I opened the door and it was Greg. Of course, I was not too disappointed. Kris would be along shortly and I always enjoyed looking at Greg. I signed for the food and pushed the cart inside for him. I winked and then let him know I would see him the following afternoon. He said he was going to be working and I let him know I would be ordering sausage and would be alone. He smiled.

Before we had even checked under all the service tray lids there was another knock at the door. I walked to the door and saw Kris standing there. It was good to see him. He had walked into my world and been instrumental in many ways to my success. His appearance was comfortable. I gave him a hug and invited him in for breakfast.

If I had smoked anything that morning I might have questioned what I would see next. These two youngsters were diggin' on each other. It was cute to

watch, but I would have to make sure Kris understood Cassie and Amy Jo didn't need to know about certain parts of my business. I could go into all that with him later that day.

We all chowed down. Then Amy Jo put Colton down for a quick nap. The four of us grown folks burned up some strawberry cough sativa that Kris had. It was pretty nice grass and tasted awesome. There was just enough to get all four of us feeling nice without making us all stupid.

I surprised the girls by handing them each a thousand in cash. I announced that Kris and I were going to go look into a couple of business opportunities and he would be working with us going forward. They asked if they could go shop and were pleased to hear that was the plan. I asked them to drive us by the bank and to Westside Dodge on their way. They, of course, agreed. After stopping at the bank, they dropped us off at the dealership. We all agreed to go to dinner at the Opus later.

After we were dropped off at the dealership, we began to walk the used car lot looking at the C300 Sedans. For a moment or two it was just the two of us. I accused him of being hot for Amy Jo. He denied it. I laughed and reminded him that I was the boss, and that he needed to leave her alone for a while. Then we saw the salesman approaching.

Kris was laughing while reminding me that he knew I was the boss when we found out that our salesman's name was Troy. Troy was a likeable guy

knowledgeable and attentive. The three of us test drove three C series sedans, a beige, a silver, and a black one. After Troy went through all the options and features, it was the silver one that best served my needs. I coughed up thirty thousand and Kris and I were on our way.

I had Kris drive and as we sped away toward the shop, I explained to him that this was his company car. He smiled at that news, but was a little edgy about heading to the massage office. Once again I reminded him that I was indeed still the boss and that it wasn't optional.

"I know, I know", he said, but went on to mention that Ciara and Andrea were both shitty to him when he said he was coming to work for me.

As we pulled up to front of the office, I instructed Kris to sit in the car while I went in. As soon as I walked in it was on.

"So now you just take our employees?" Andrea exclaimed.

"Yeah, what kind of shit is that Petra? Ciara added.

"Excuse me ladies, really! Am I hearing this shit correctly? Let me see, Andrea, so now you just finger bang and French kiss my girlfriend when I take the two of you out? You mean that kind of shit, huh, Ciara? Also, I was unaware that there would be a problem with me choosing to promote one of my employees and to allow the purchase of this business.

Is there a fucking problem here ladies? I thought that I was being pretty cool here. I haven't heard from you two, but based on past trends, I figure that you will want to see me later. Let's all be professional here ladies. I am still the boss until you two pay me one hundred twenty-five thousand! So do you two trifling bitches want to fuck with me some more or what?" I unloaded.

"No Petra. I'm sorry, we're sorry." Ciara said motioning to Andrea.

"Yeah, it just kind of came out, but you didn't have to call us trifling; did you?" Andrea said.

"Your right. I did not have to say it, but if the shoe fits! Understand girls I want to go on without hard feelings, however, what happened was a slap in the face. Do you two have your money ready to go for the business? I responded.

"Yes we're ready." Ciara answered while Andrea nodded.

"I will draw it up and bring the contract over. You will officially take over in six weeks. I will make my full salary for this and next month. Ciara I will need the apartment this afternoon and then I will leave the key. Do we all understand here?"

They nodded in affirmation and I walked out the door. I was done there.

I walked back out to the silver sedan, and Kris and I pulled away from the "Service for men" office for the last time. Everything else would be taken care of at

the attorney's offices. Kris asked me how things had gone. I told him that all things considered, things went well. He asked what had happened. I explained about the tittie bar, Ciara and Andrea, meeting Amy Jo, hiring her, the condo, etc. etc. I got him caught up to speed and let him know what I was thinking as far as business went, legal and illegal. After all that, I told him to drive by the condo. He did, of course.

He was blown away by the outside and you could tell he was kind of getting off on all of it. He was moving up with me and it was obvious that he was very happy about all of this. He was also really into the whole strip club deal.

"Hey, Petra! I know a great location for a tittie bar if you want to look at it?"

"I think so Kris, but I would like for you to refer to it as a gentlemen's club. We are actually going to bring class to the topless bar business here in OKC."

"OK Boss."

"All right then set it up for this afternoon around four. For now, though, I want you to drive us back over to the Skirvin."

"Got it Boss Lady."

He turned us that way.

When we got there the room was empty. We put the room service cart out into the hall, and I handed him five hundred to go get the Chrysler's windows murdered out and pick me up a safe. I told him to

come back and pick me up at the room by three forty-five. He left.

I called Victor and made arrangements to stop by his house to visit. He would need to be brought up to speed. He had once told me that one of the things he really liked about me was that I was open with him and he could tell there was no dishonesty in me. He loved it when the people that worked with him kept him in the loop. I was not about to let Victor down.

As I drove over to his place, I was nearly one hundred per cent sure that he had my back, but just like anyone moving money, I was getting the usual feelings of doubt associated with business shake ups. The attitude that I heard from the girls was a little unexpected. The other thing, it was all still unfinished. I was certain those two were going to pull something soon. Hell, I need to stop this thinking. I might just be paranoid, but just because you're paranoid doesn't mean they're not out to get you.

As I pulled up the drive to his nearby country home, I thought about the first time I had driven the Z-28 to have a really heavy talk with Victor, and that night long ago that had Marco dead from his own dishonesty and greed. Since then, I had enjoyed a relationship with Victor that I thought was one of mutual respect and appreciation. I hoped that was still the case. For some reason the fact that Andrea had introduced us bothered me. I pulled up to the front doors and got out.

The double doors opened up as I reached for the doorbell.

"Hello Senora. I hear you have had some issues. Come in my young friend. Let us solve them together. We will sit together and have a whiskey rocks and talk."

I smiled at him and was sure that what I would get from him was honest. I was also certain that he had news for me.

The first thing I did was ask if I could get twelve kilos for the two hundred thousand dollars that I had brought with me.

"Ah as beautiful as you are, you have never let yourself be confused about what really turns me on my old friend. You will get fourteen!"

I was surprised since the twelve was already asking for a price break. I was surprised but glad as hell too. I filled him in on everything that was transpiring with and around me. He laughed at my lover's spat as he called it. He then went on to let me know that Ciara and Andrea had approached him telling lies about me and trying to go around me. He told them twenty-four per bird and they flew.

I smiled when I realized that he was protecting the twenty-two I was charging. He saw my smile and warned me not to be too confident. He would keep his ear to the ground for me. He warned that even though the price I was giving them was good, he felt they

would be shopping it around. He was also nearly certain that they were going to make a move on me.

He said, "I saw so much jealousy in them Senora Novakova."

I always loved it when he spoke to me this way. He let me know that Miguel would deliver my gym bag to the apartment in one hour. I hugged him and left.

I stopped and picked up some crystalized B on my way to the apartment. I was going to use my old trick one last time. I would sell this through and keep out two hundred thousand. That plus what I had out would be my new beginning. The other one seventy-four would bring my safe deposit back up to a cool million. The money from the business and my two month's severance pay would have my bank account back up to around a quarter million. I felt strongly that this would be where I needed to be to begin this next evolution of Petra.

Chapter 31

When I got to the apartment it was painfully obvious that Andrea was already moved in. Wow! I really couldn't believe it when I saw all my clothes had been placed in the entrance closet. I thought that was tacky as hell. Anyway, I broke out the Pyrex and went to work. As I was washing up the pans, I wondered just what those two might be up to. I took all my things out to the Camaro and waited on Miguel.

After Miguel came and then left, I went to work turning the fourteen kilos into seventeen. When the last of it had been cooled and bagged, I washed up all the dishes, dried them and put them up. I called Andrea and asked her to bring the forty-four thousand for the two kilos they needed to the apartment. She agreed.

I had placed all of the drugs other than the two birds that they wanted to fly in the car along with my other things and I decided to peek around a little. I thought there might be a chance that something would tip me off as to what these two, getting more evil by the minute bitches, were up to.

On the bed I found a book of guns. You know one of those books that could be purchased out of the

back of guns and ammo. There was a page marker in it
marking a page on noise suppressors for medium
caliber pistols. Silencers, what were these two little
gangsters thinking. I could not believe they were really
going to try to kill me. Maybe this was all coincidence,
maybe not. Could these two have now fashioned
themselves as little Scarface gangsters. Somehow I had
become what stood between them and the crown.

I put everything right back where it was and sat
on the couch waiting for Andrea. When she arrived our
visit was without event. She betrayed nothing of their
plot, if they had one. She paid me, and I left, stopping
by the bank to put about fifteen thousand back in the
safe deposit box.

I called Audra when I got back to the room and
double checked to make sure all was still on for the
next day. It was. Then I stuffed the gym bag into the
in room safe and laid down on the couch to wait for
Kris. Sitting there alone with my thoughts, I found it
very difficult to fathom that Ciara and Andrea were
thinking about killing me. Difficult or not, I could not
afford to not consider it. It sucks to think that a couple
of women, who by my design accidental or not had
accumulated some wealth and comfort were now ready
to kill me. It sucks to think that greed and envy were
invading with totality two relationships that I had
always treated with love and respect. I had nurtured
these relationships while treating them with an integrity
that was in all probability never reciprocated. With a
certain degree of sadness, I chuckled as I

acknowledged that it was more likely these women had fallen prey to the seven deadly sins than it was that they had not. I would be ready if this was indeed my reality. Do people suck or what? Greed and envy, thou shalt not covet!

The door opened and there were Amy Jo, Cassie, and Colton. Straggling in behind, carrying the bags was Kris. They had run into each other in the parking lot and from the looks of it, Kris had gotten the worst end of the deal. After a moment or two of watching the ladies show off what they had purchased, I indicated to Kris that it was time to go. He nodded and the two of us assured the girls we would see them soon for our trip North to the Opus steakhouse. We all needed a fun, soothing night. Tomorrow was a big day and it looked more and more like there would be plenty of those to come.

As we were walking out to the car, Kris began to fill me in. The current owner of the club, The Platinum Room, was a man named Benjamin DeChico or Bennie. The club was located in the little city of Valleybrook, an odd little city within a city. About one-mile square, Valleybrook consisted of five strip clubs, a few other businesses, a neighborhood, and a sedentary and predatory police force made up of washouts, has-beens and never-weres that made their living pulling over bar patrons after chalking their tires to see who had been inside the longest.

From what I could gather, he was trying to say that it had potential and had at one time been the

premier spot to be if you were a dancer, but had recently lost out to clubs like "night dreams and the playground". Between the rise of places like that and the platinum room's series of poor owners, there had been a real shift in the way the strip club entertainment dollars had been spent recently. In other words, the place was in decline but reusable.

We pulled up and the entrance had real potential. It was obvious if this was representative of the rest of the club that at one time it had been the shit. I was getting a little bit excited as we got out of the car and walked up to the door. I could see things coming together in my head as we walked in and I looked around; this place has possibilities.

Chapter 32

If the bar had potential, the owner did not.
"Bennie" DeChico was something else entirely. If
there ever was a human being that could have done the
name salacious worm credit it was Bennie. Bennie was
a creepy little man with greasy, thinning hair and beady
little, extremely dilated eyes. In fact, it may have been
an insult to the character from Jabba's fortress I
mentioned previously. One thing about Bennie was
that between his appearance and his manner, all of this
place's problems were blatantly obvious. The only
question now was the price.

Once I got past this guy's leering stare, I found
out that he was in immediate trouble with his suppliers,
twenty-seven thousand dollars down. He also had
personal issues to the tune of about forty thousand
dollars. For sixty thousand dollars I could own the
whole thing. I could have the rights to the lease, an
agreement with two years left on it. I could have all the
club's debt. I could also have all of its potential. We
agreed that I could take over in two days assuming that
my lawyer approved the papers his lawyer drew up. I
was in the bar business. This place would be great!

On the way back to the Skirvin, Kris and I were stoked. I saw real money making potential there. We would call it "The Platinum Lady". For Kris, I think he was just happy to be a part of something like this. His pecker liked the whole idea more than his brain did. I called the room, and since the girls were ready, we agreed to meet at the steakhouse. I had big news to share with them.

Opus was a nice white table cloth kind of place and I wanted to elevate these folks image of themselves and their place in the world. I don't care what anyone says, if you act as though you are, you will become; and with regular meals at nice places like Opus, you will begin to see yourself as though you are one of the beautiful people. These two women and our male compatriot Kris all had class within them. Class is one thing that can't be taught. Sometimes, though, it is there just waiting to be brought out. This group would shine. Kris was already tested and loyal. Amy Jo and her sweet mom Cassie were good people who had been thrown a life preserver before they were destroyed by theirs as well as the desperation of others.

We all ordered and I added a bottle of Caymus Cellars 1998 cabernet sauvignon. It was an occasion for a toast and I had other things to discuss as well. We were into a new business and what they would not know tonight was that I had decided to keep my massage business as well. Why not? I built it!

At dinner, I announced our newest acquisition to the girls and we had a toast to that as well as several

other announcements. Other than the news about "The Platinum Lady", there was college. Kris and Amy Jo were to attend classes full time and work part time. Amy Jo was going to take accounting and business management courses. Kris was to do business management as well as criminal justice and security courses. In his case, there was a little of the adage "know your enemy". Another great phrase is "chance favors the prepared mind". We would be prepared and I would be paying the bills to make it possible. We went through the rundown for the following day. The girls were to meet Kris at the condo about 8 A.M. We had a new address. They were to meet the furniture movers and the nerd squad from Best Electronics. I would be around later after checking out and meeting a couple of people. The day after that, I would take possession of the club.

The next morning, right after Amy Jo and Cassie went to meet Audra, I rolled a big bowl of shit and ordered some sausage. I needed to fuck and I had young Greg's hot body in mind. It wasn't afternoon yet, but I bet he would deliver the meat.

I was edgy, playing with my clit until I almost got off then bringing it back. After about twenty minutes of this there was a knock at the door. I was dripping wet and horny as hell. I opened the door. It was Greg. He smiled and brought in the cart. I asked him if he did a thorough job when delivering the meat. He smiled and I hit my knees. After unzipping him I pulled out his useable tool and wrapped my lips around

it. He tensed up and blew his wad in like five seconds. To make matters worse, he got all embarrassed and before I could help him get back in the game he stammered about work or some shit and ran off. What a fucking waste of effort!

I locked the door behind him and finished myself off in the shower. I came hard and was still left hungry and dissatisfied. I didn't give myself much of a chance by expecting so much from Greg. He would have had to have been Peter North or some other super stamina porn God to satisfy the buildup I had given him.

I packed up and checked out of the hotel. I made a stop or two before I went to see Victor. He greeted me enthusiastically with a fatherly hug before welcoming me into his home. He had lemonade brought to us and then indicated that the two of us should stay sober for the conversation. He had news.

My off the wall suspicions were correct. What I was blown away by was they had been shopping for a hitter for over two weeks now and I thought that this was some break up bullshit. They did not plan on paying for the business. They did not plan for me to live that long. Well if imitation is the greatest form of flattery, why don't I feel flattered? These bitches wanted to be me! Well, fuck them!

Victor and I sat and talked for a little longer. We discussed some possibilities and agreed to speak again in about a week. I told him how much I appreciated him.

As always with such grace he says, "Oh no Senorita. It is I who am in your debt. You are, how do you say, inspiring!"

Ah! He was as silver tongued a devil as they came, but genuine as well. It was so good to have him as a friend.

I stopped by my lawyer's office. Tom had received the paperwork on the exchange of ownership for "The Platinum Room." He also had the paperwork to file the name change to "The Platinum Lady". I left him a check with instructions to fax a copy of the check to that creep Bennie's lawyers. I would take possession at midnight. The club was mine.

I left Tom's office and drove to the condo. I was excited as hell to be nearing the end of this week. There were problems ahead, but I was looking forward to some peace before, and hopefully, afterwards. Besides, I had dealt with scarier things than this present danger.

As I pulled up, it looked like everybody had arrived. The place looked quite busy and it pleased me to see the beginning of normalcy here at the new digs. Even Kris was excited and he didn't even get to live here. It was a lovely place. I walked closer and could feel all the giddy little fun feelings of anticipation that go with a cool new place to live. Especially when it is the first place I've owned. How cool is that?

I didn't want to disturb much. I greeted the ladies and hugged the baby. I could tell I was going to

get attached to these folks. God, I hope they don't let me down. I tip the delivery guys a hundred dollars each and tell Kris to go get the Mercedes. Then we have to get to the club.

When we get to the car, I slip Kris a couple hundred bucks to pick up some basic groceries for the girls, drop them off, and then meet me at the club. He nods and takes off. I start the 'cedes and do the same.

I pull up to the door and get out. A young man that I would later learn was named Charles walked up and said, "Ma'am you can't park here!"

I answered, "Yes I can young man. My name is Petra Novakova and I am the new head bitch in charge. Park my car kid and then come inside." I tossed him the keys and walked in. To avoid making a scene in the doorway as I entered, I paid the three-dollar cover charge.

Chapter 33

I stepped just barely into the bar and waited on the kid. He came inside and almost ran right into me before he got himself stopped.

"My name is Charles." He said.

"Great! Nice to meet you. Give me my keys and bring me your manager. I want to talk to the guy that answers to Bennie." I demanded.

Charles scurried off to find the bar manager and I find my way to a table close to the doors where I was able to be more subtle.

As I sat there waiting I was curious exactly what I had working for me. The kind of person I had in my employ would either be great help, or a curse that would need to go. The second possibility would mean that I would have a lot more work ahead. Hopefully, I had a winner here tucked away and stifled by Bennie's stupidity.

I saw Charles approach with a tall, broad shouldered fellow with a blond ponytail.

"Hi! My name is Gene." The tall man said.

I responded, "Hello Gene. I am Petra Novakova. At midnight I will become the owner of this establishment. Are you the bar manager?"

"It is a pleasure to meet you. Yes, I am the bar manager."

"Gene, have Charles bring us some beers and sit down."

"OK." He motions to Charles who disappears and quickly returns with a bucket of suds.

I take a long drink of Coors. "This beer needs to be much colder, Gene."

"Bennie, Ma'am", he responds blaming his boss for the warm beer

"Fuck Bennie. Go turn the coolers down and ice the beer down better. After you do that, tell Bennie to come turn over the keys and get the fuck out"!

"Yes Mam!"

I watch as he goes behind the bar and then up the stars. Bennie comes back down the stairs with him and approaches me yelling.

"Who do you think you are Bimbo?"

"Whoa, easy there asshole unless you want to find another buyer. Shut the fuck up. Hand over the keys and get the fuck out, now! You're not needed here anymore."

He sat there staring at me, furious. Then he handed over the keys. Head hung he walked out. Fuck him.

"Wow", Gene said.

"Wow what? I asked.

"Just Bennie knows people and I haven't ever seen any one talk to him like that before."

"Like I said Gene, fuck Bennie! Look, I don't take shit and I am not about to start taking it off the likes of Bennie. Gene, this is about us now. Do you get the fuck out too, or do you want to stick around? If you do, tell me what you need from me right now and what you think needs to be done to improve all this?"

I motioned around me to the unattractive room full of potential. Then shrugged my shoulders as if to say, "balls in your court".

"Hey, Lady Boss, I'm staying. The first thing we need is to pay our booze bill. We can't get anything, and nearly no one comes for titties and water!"

"Are you talking about the twenty-seven thousand dollars?"

"Twenty-nine." He says wincing.

"Here, call our distributor to pick this up."

I pull out my check book and write the guy a forty-thousand-dollar check.

"Who do I make this out to?" I ask.

Gene looks at the check and takes off to make the call. He is already looking less stressed.

Gene walks back up to the table. "OK Lady Boss. That was so right on time and one month late.

We literally were going to be out of booze tomorrow night. Ms. Novakova I really think this place can be special if I can ever quit having to worry about just keeping the doors open."

"It's Petra, Gene, and those days are over. I want you to tell me all your ideas for this place, right this second. Keep in mind before you begin that you will be held accountable for all your words and your value to me will come, in part, from your next statement."

We began to speak back and forth with him beginning, of course. I liked the guy's ideas and the passion he had for the business. He had vision and energy. He also had the exuberance of no longer suppressed hope. It was obvious that this place had been hobbled and bled by Bennie the worm.

As we walked around the bar, Gene giving me the tour, we clicked. We fed off each other's ideas. I thought about a huge storage room being turned into a VIP lounge for lap dances. He thought of mirrored walls lined with plush throne styled chairs and stripper poles in front of each one. I thought about plush faux leather pit groups on each side wall. He envisioned them on pedestal flooring with thick carpeting. I saw pebbles in the sinks and urinals. He saw newspapers on the walls in cases above them.

Things continued to click and click. Flat screen TV's everywhere, multiple sports channels, and playboy television. A huge nearly full length mahogany bar with a gray field stone façade. Import

beer on tap as well as the domestics. Reduce the pool tables from four to two and replace with shuffle board tables. He mentioned nice faux velvet chairs. I mentioned only glass ashtrays in our club. New Carpet! New tables! Television in the bathrooms. A public bathroom for women, and a ladies night too!

We sat back down at the table. We were both excited about working with each other and it took us a moment to calm down and catch our breath. We had a sorry looking waitress bring us a couple of beers. This brought us to another topic of conversation, the girls. Some of them had to go and I made it clear ugly bitches and cellulite were out. Period!

Chapter 34

Strategy was simple, slowly find ways to fire them as we lowered capacity through the next several months for construction. He was to get three estimates for each project and bring them to me. I would give him cash on a case by case basis. When done we would close for one month to finish remodeling reopening as the platinum lady. By then all the ugly girls should be gone. We should have consistent uniforms for wait and bar staff. We would entice all the best talent in town by offering a fifty dollar per night pay for coming in and dancing. After two months, we would do away with it and use the money to put in a decent buffet and raise our cover to ten dollars, buffet included.

The last two things were the unused balcony space and his status of employment. They were both simple discussions to have. Gene would also convert all the unused balcony space to exclusive balconies and they were to be wonderfully appointed as well.

The second topic was easy. I liked the way he thought. He would be audited by an accountant that I paid and selected each week. He was to receive a twenty per cent raise effective immediately. Lastly

upon completion of these projects and the grand re-opening he was to become twenty per cent owner.

He was as excited as a fat kid in a candy store. I only hoped that I was not wrong about him, and that he would also show some loyalty. Seems like that was a tough quality to locate and reel in. I was still positive; however, that an open hand would hold more than a closed fist and that if found before spirits were crushed by greed of others there were still many out there willing to prosper through honest work.

As I got up to leave, Gene stopped me. It seemed that there was one more problem that I should know about. The owner of two of the dives up the street, Dicky Abner, wasn't going to like any of this. He apparently was a self-absorbed small time wise guy with an over inflated sense of self. This guy sounds all too familiar. Was there like a full time factory making sure that there was always a supply of these cock suckers? No need to respond. It was rhetorical. The story is that Bennie had to pay this guy to operate in Valleybrook. Gene didn't know exactly how he enforced all this, but he seemed to focus his efforts on keeping these places low rent. He also had two girls selling dope on the premises for him.

I was already looking for legitimacy and I had already planned on a no dope policy for this place. Those two had to go now. Other than that, we would have to do two things. One, play it by ear. Two, install a comprehensive camera heavy surveillance system.

"Fuck this guy," I thought to myself. I am a hell of a lot tougher than Bennie. What a puss.

I let Gene know that I would have Kris come in later to talk to him. Also that Kris would find a couple of security guys and a system and get all that going for him. We were not going to tuck and run from Dicky Abner. Not even for one day. Fuck that! I could tell that this attitude excited Gene as well as concerned him. He would learn to have a little faith in his new Boss Lady. I left to go to my new home.

I was excited about it all. It was wild having my whole life change inside of a week. You know, I have experienced more violent, more shocking, more dramatic changes in my life than this one. I had been through the radical change story before. I had wilted at times, but I never died. Now not only had I proven to be able to survive, but I have shown I could thrive. There was a healthy amount of concern for my situation. There was no real fear of my enemies anymore. Fear has been replaced by a calm genuine confidence. I knew that I would come through this. I was certain that I would be victorious. I was only almost thirty years old but I was a seasoned veteran where survival was concerned.

When I arrived back at the condo everything was pretty much where it belonged. They had fried up a feast of prepared frozen food products. There were stuffed crabs, corn dogs, frozen shoestring potatoes, tater tots, chicken tenders, fish sticks, and hush puppies. All that and ice cream with pecan pie for

dessert. Our little group was coming together and the attraction between Amy Jo and Kris was super evident as well. We all had a blast watching blue rays on our new home theater and taking turns getting the munchies and munching. Cassie and I sat and alternated between laughing at the awkward young adults in front of us while they tried to express that they might just want more than a fuck. When that was not entertaining us we were smiling at Colton. I found myself completely entranced by this little man and his easy, knowing and curious smile. What I would give to have this free, easy, simple innocence again. It would be lovely. I guess in some strange way I envied the little gorgeous shit. I would at that moment have protected his innocence with my life. Over all, the evening was fabulous and the sleep my mattress assisted with was awesome.

I found Kris in the living room on the couch the next morning sleeping. I woke him up and had him wake up the ladies. We cooked some breakfast, and then Kris and I left to go see the Lua brothers. I reminded the girls to call and check on enrollment dates. I also gave them another thousand for more food, counter top appliances and cookware. They had their day ahead of them and we had ours.

On the way to see the Lua brothers, guys Kris knew, I called Gene and asked him to meet us at the club around noon. When we got to their apartment in Norman, I could see immediately what Kris was thinking. These guys were humongous. Fucking

humongous! The door opened and there was Paulie Lua. I mean to say that was all you saw. There was a door jam and then there was Paulie. At about 6'6" in height and about three hundred pounds, Paulie was the perfect harmony of terrifying and pleasant. He stood there with a huge welcoming smile and kind voice saying, "Hey, is this the Boss Lady you were telling me about? Come on in bro!

Thank the lord these guys were nice because his brother, Kalo, was even bigger. It turns out they had gotten grant money to attend the University of Oklahoma and they had partial scholarships for weight lifting as well. They were Samoans, and were very convincing intimidators. They would be able to do it with big, polite smiles as well. The kindness was genuine. I could tell that they truly were nice guys. The intimidation factor was genuine. These two just oozed strength and power.

After a nice little talk, it seemed like they might like working security for me. They needed easy, consistent cash. They were well suited to it and they loved the company of women. Last, but not least, they loved titties. They could work five days a week for a bill fifty a night cash. I asked them to meet us there in black T-shirts about one that afternoon.

Kris found a surveillance system with eighty cameras and a company to install it for thirty thousand. They would also take cash. They agreed to meet us there that afternoon as well. We headed to the club.

We walked into the nearly empty space. It smelled of stale smoke and beer. Just under those smells I could smell money. I could smell it and through the lenses of my dreamer's eyes I could see it. I could see the faint remains of fun times past here among the dead air. I could see the vision of fun times future. A real fun gentlemen's club where everyone matters, the owner, the employer, the customer and the dancer. Everybody can get what they want. We would sell the dream. We would have the kind of place where dreams were fulfilled. At least for a little while.

I was giving Kris, and his imagination, the tour of the new Platinum Lady when Gene joined us smiling. He let me know that Dicky's girls, Lila and Ava were terminated. Also, the club had taken in thirteen hundred twenty-six dollars the night before. He had taken it home. He did not want to deposit the cash into the bar's account since that was Bennie's. We would need to see about getting another account set up later. I was expecting things to get kind of lively here pretty quickly. Everything else would need to wait. I had an announcement to make.

Chapter 35

I asked the guys to brew some coffee. I sat smoking a cig and ashing into the cheap ashtray that would soon be replaced. The fellas came and sat down with me and we talked. I let Gene know that the surveillance guys would be there soon and that I wanted to introduce Kris's security guys to him. Gene asked about the security guys and the two of us let that linger. We had already decided to let their appearance speak for itself.

Those two got to discussing football and then the security systems company showed up. There were three of them. Now there were five adult adolescents walking around somehow figuring out how to lay out the cameras by talking about Adrian Peterson and Ben Roethlisberger. Occasionally they would drift back in time and a name like Bob Griese or Fran Tarkenton would waft across the air.

The five of them walked up the stairs to the balconies. Only a minute or so passed before the doors flew open. Just as I expected, Dicky Abner. He was a tall, rangy guy. He looked oily and as he got closer smelled of patchouli. He had an air of irritability about him and I expected that he spent a lot of his time

irritated. He had a thick poof of hair that was probably treated with a pomade or brill cream. Just a dab will do you, Dicky.

He was not alone. He had a couple of goons with him. They walked up on me quickly and Dicky's voice was loud when he said, "You must be the broad that had my girls canned last night! You don't know who you are messing with, do ya?"

What a trip! I guess I was about to find out, huh? These guys were all so predictable.

"You must be Dicky Abner or should I call you Richard. I assume you are referring to Lila and Ava. I was informed that they were selling drugs for you while here. We don't do that anymore. Yes, I had Gene terminate them! Oh, by the way Dicky, don't bother telling me how much your shake down will be. It doesn't matter. We won't be paying!" I finished and sat smugly through the little pause before he came back loudly while shaking his fist at me.

"Look lady I don't think you understand. You better have plenty of muscle to talk to me like that!"

I could not have drawn it up better. As soon as he said muscle, the doors opened and in walked the Lua brothers.

"Dicky I would like to introduce you to plenty of muscle. Kalo, Paulie, Mr. Abner was just threatening me. Please show him and his boys to the door. Also, explain to him since this place is not about

drugs or prostitution we won't need his services, and we won't be paying his fees."

As I finished, the gargantuan Lua brothers already had their giant mitts on Dicky and his goons.

"Yes Ms. Novakova we will deliver the message," they said.

From the sound of Dicky and his boys being bounced off the doors and the delay between their exit and the Lua brothers' re-entry, I had no doubt the message had been delivered.

The Luas walked back up and Kalo said, "This job is already more fun than I thought it would be. Hey, Boss Lady, you OK?"

I laughed. "Very OK. Thanks!"

The other guys came down the stairs. "Hey! What's all the commotion?"

I looked over at them and said, "You guys missed it! Dicky Abner was just telling us all how uninterested he is in extorting the bar anymore. Right guys?"

"Right Boss Lady" Paulie said.

He, Kalo, and I started to laugh.

The guys from the security company, Gene and Kris were all just looking at the three of us like we were out of minds. They would be laughing too if they had seen it all. Then the four guys, other than Kris, were staring for different reasons. Now they were just

trying to take the Lua brothers all in. I understand, side by side they make you wish you had a wide angle lens.

"Gene, these guys are your new bouncers. I just watched them in action. They're good. Very good!"

Poor guy. He just stood there in shock looking at these fellas in disbelief.

"Hey bro! I'm Paulie and this is Kalo. We are the Lua brothers. Nice to meet you."

"Nice to meet you," Gene managed to say. "Good to have you aboard."

I handed the surveillance guys an envelope of cash and got a receipt. I told the Luas to look around while Gene, Kris and myself ran to the back.

The three of us went to set up a new business account. Our mood was light, especially after I told them the whole story about meeting Dicky Abner. I was certain he would be back around. I was, however, just as certain if would be a while before we heard from him again. After we got the account opened, I had the guys drop me off at the condo before they went back to work things out at the club.

Chapter 36

The next several weeks really allowed things to settle in. I was comfortable that radical or not, I had made some good moves and collected some good people to add to my family. I had been pampering myself with manicures, pedicures and spa facials. I found that Cassie was super cool to hang with. She was a mother figure and a sister figure to boot. I found the hours I spent with her to be soothing, and I truly sensed that the time she spent with me left her feeling cool as well. Even her skin had a glow to it that said a big weight had been lifted.

Colton was literally the coolest guy there was. He left me believing there was hope for men. His cool pee-wee like confidence and his smiling face, complete with huge baby blues, left me happily mesmerized every time. I was pretty sure he liked me too. At least that is my story and I'm sticking to it.

Amy Jo was a treat to watch. She was enrolled in classes and with a little help from her friends, she was getting a last little taste of being a teenager. It looked good on her too. From a business stand point she was proving that she might be a good investment.

At least her grades were good. She and Cassie did a fantastic job of managing the household for me.

I formed a company, Novakova Enterprises. It was to be a parent company for both "the Platinum Lady and A Service for Men." It would also umbrella everything else I found myself into later. I had Amy Jo using a simple program to keep track of Novakova enterprises. I would let the two grow with each other. I brought in an independent to audit the bitches over at "A Service for Men" and "The Platinum Lady". I also had her audit Amy Jo once per month. It kept the honest and dishonest alike, pretty honest, and it helped Amy Jo and Gene grow into their new roles slowly.

My bank account after being nearly completely depleted was filling back up. I was still picking up around ten grand per month with the massage business. A bonus, despite all the club's problems, it was still operating with a profit, and I was picking up about six thousand a month there as well.

I was paying all my bills and Kris, Amy Jo and Cassie in cash. On top of all that, I was allocating funds for remodel and repair with cash as well. Doing all that, I was still climbing. There was an even million in one safety deposit box and a second one had been started with twenty grand in it. I also had floor safes at both the condo and the club with ten grand cash in them, just in case. You know oops money so to speak.

Ciara and Andrea were getting down right icy even though we had done two more deals. There was no more polite conversation with those two trifling

bitches when they purchased the last time. Hell, they even somehow managed to make me feel like I had inconvenienced them by selling them good shit for a good price. There had been no more talk of buying the business. Of course not. Why buy something you are going to steal from a dead woman. Those two's true colors had certainly begun to show.

Thinking I should pay them a visit, I stopped by the office one morning. They were certainly surprised. I definitely was made to feel like I was not welcome in their litter box. Talk about catty. These two were the picture next to the definition in the Webster's dictionary. Since I was made to feel very uncomfortable, I thought it would only be right to return the favor. I let them know I had a buyer interested for a quarter of a million, and furthermore, I would not think of selling for a dime less. They were told that the buyer was looking to take possession in approximately three months. Then I left without waiting for a response.

I was laughing my ass off all the way through the next week while I took care of my cash customers. I thought it might be time for another sit down with Victor. I needed to know what he knew and I needed to arrange another drop as well. It was funny as hell thinking of those two trying to figure out who my fictitious buyer was. Time for then to feel a little heat. Let them sweat a little. You know, it is easy to criticize and hate from the cheap seats. Time they figure out that weary is the head on which the crown sits. If you

want to be the queen, you have to actually kill the
queen, not just talk about it.

Chapter 37

After a good night's rest, I went to see Victor. He was magnanimous and cordial as always. He poured us each a Don Julio blue and pineapple juice. "Your girls are still up to their little tricks my dear, sweet Petra. How do you say? They are determined. No?"

I let him know that I had already let them know about my new mythical buyer. He laughed and said he would have liked to have been a fly on the wall the minute after I left. After he mentioned it, I had to agree that it did seem like it might have been funny. We finished our drinks and enjoyed flirting with each other.

The conversation was easy between us as always. Even when I brought up an exit strategy and legitimacy he remained calm. I would be less than honest if I were to tell you that this calmness didn't concern me at all. It did, and for more than just a minute too. Victor was an extremely powerful man. He was much more powerful than I could have imagined when we first met. Also I would be stupid to assume that he was only as powerful as I now thought. I suspected that I was a small fish in his world, and that in reality, I was someone he would normally have

almost nothing to do with. I was a small, "pet" fish, who for his reasons, whatever they were, he embraced. I had the impression that there was a very loose family connection with Andrea, this being the tiny little original connection to that shithead named Marco.

All that said, I was either screwed or not and that was already determined. I could only conduct myself the way I felt like I should and trust my instincts. My instincts said that where I was concerned, Victor was genuine. I had to trust that. I had to hope that was true. I also had to make a deal so I handed Victor a bag of money. He smiled and agreed to have it delivered by a fellow in a delivery uniform and truck to the condo. As I walked out the door, he said, "Get your head up. It will all work out. Watch".

Maybe he could sense that I needed reassurance. Maybe he was setting me up. Either way I felt hopefully relieved.

Things went along pretty normally for a couple of months. The only real change was that Ciara and Andrea quit buying anything a few weeks after my announcement. Based on their feelings towards me and what I knew, anything less would be really strange. They were not really a big part of that piece of my business anymore anyway.

Everything was going better than planned, and much better than could reasonably be expected. With the obvious exception of Ciara and Andrea, my meth business was going well. Sales were up and costs were down. What more could anyone possible want. Hell,

even my drop offs and pickups were as smooth as silk. Like I said, even better than expected.

Kris had found two reliable and useful guys to work with and spell the Lua brothers. The security surveillance system was working well. Gene had been able to use it to spot behavior that management should be aware of as well as some behavior that made some problems, fat, ugly, and otherwise, easy to terminate with cause.

It required only the smallest amount of imagination to envision the direction the club was headed. We were getting close to shutting down for four to five weeks to finish the remodel before the grand reopening. The buzz was good. The girls were getting excited and the rumor, which by the way was true, about us paying the finest bitches in town to come dance upon reopening was causing a pleasant stir for dancers all over town. A stir below the waist where it counts; in the pockets! There were other club owners who were already pissed off about that and that was good. Hate is many times an expression of flattery.

The rumors of how plush and cool we would look did not even begin to do justice to how slick the truth would be. Even the inadequate talk had industry people talking. Better yet was the only thing that really mattered, the customers were getting excited.

I had kept up with overall expenses in cash and had a little over three hundred thousand put up in safe deposit box number two to finish the project. "The Platinum Lady" was going to be awesome. I was

raking in ten Gs a month out of the bitch now. The sky was the limit.

Cassie and Amy Jo helped me as much as I helped them, maybe even more. Where little Colton was concerned, it was a no brainer. He made me a better person every time I was lucky enough to hang out with his gorgeous little self. The four of us spent our nights acting just like the family we were becoming. Amy Jo's grades were stellar, a 4.0 G.P.A. Cassie was a glowing grandmother and I was glad to be there with them. In some ways, there was healing occurring in me in places that a few months prior I would have told you no longer existed. I had quit struggling for or against wholeness and in the process of letting go I was experiencing the process of becoming. And I liked it!

"A Service for Men" was doing more than holding its own. I had made twenty-five thousand in the last two months in the massage business. An area of concern for me still, however, Ciara and Andrea had become way too nice to me. They were no longer buying dope from me, and they had been inquiring about having me killed. The business they ran for me, the one they wanted to purchase, was doing better than ever. Now their attitude had shifted dramatically from icy to syrupy sweet! What the fuck was going on here? The cool, confidence that had been the new me was, as far as these two bitches were concerned, becoming a touch unnerved. There were no signs of unraveling.

Of course, that never means that it doesn't feel that way moment to moment.

Everything clipped along for the next six weeks or so. Right before the shut down for the final remodeling, something really strange happened. Ciara and Andrea did not show up for work one day. I called the apartment and their phones didn't answer. I went by the apartment. No answer. After a day of trying to reach them and getting no response, I reported it to the police as missing persons.

The police showed up at the office and asked me so many questions. The whole time I was thankful for that night long ago when I had been questioned by the police for two hours when Javier blew his brains out. The police were very interested in the fact that Ciara and I had been an item and had lived together. When they put that with the fact that I employed them both. Their line of questioning was aggressive and almost accusatory. Had I not already experienced a detective's aggressive and tricky tactics once I probably would have closed the doors. That wouldn't have helped anyone.

As the police were leaving, two professionally dressed women walked in the office. As I looked them over, admiring their pant suits, one of them asked for Petra. I had called Victor to let him know what had happened. He didn't know anything, but when I didn't call him back to let him know anything, these two showed up. He had sent his two nieces, Mary Anne

and Dorothy over to apply for part time work. After speaking to them briefly, they joined the team.

Thank goodness, cause these two gals were good. They were also bringing a little meth business back my way. The little bit of business that Ciara and Andrea had withheld from me before they disappeared. I wondered what happened to them, but then I gave up and assumed they had come up with another plan of action. Either way it was paying dividends for me. All three parts of my little money making empire were paying off at a slightly higher rate and we were just weeks away from the pre-reopening shutdown.

Chapter 38

Mary Anne and Dorothy seemed to catch on quickly, and any one referred by Victor was probably solid. It wasn't like I had any other viable choice. I let them have the reins under the scrutiny of a weekly audit of the legal side of that little operation. I needed to be spending my time at The Lady getting ready for her final makeover.

I apparently never became a person of interest in the disappearance of Ciara and Andrea. If I was, I never heard about it. My mind and body were where they needed to be on the reopening. I was spending a lot more time there at night really getting a feel for things. I was allowing myself to envision every last swanky, sparkling detail of every last inch of the club. The Lady was going to be my crown jewel. My empire. It was all mine! Finally, my whole life was becoming my own. I was not filled with desire for power or greed. My attitude was that it was all mine to share. That coupled with a desire to do things right. That was the gift for the customers and the dancers at "The Platinum Lady". We were going to do things right.

Gene believed in my promise to make him an owner and rightfully so. I would do as I said I would. It really showed in his work and the level of passion expressed in his attitude. He was proving to be a great call. In fact, looking back he may have been inadvertently responsible for many great things. Right now with everything else that had been happening, I was using his energy. I was feeding off of his passion. It was both seed and catalyst for mine.

Suffice it to say that things were not going to disappoint at The Lady. I was sitting in the office talking to Gene about four days before the temporary closing and guess who showed up all uninvited with his slimy self? Dicky Abner.

"Hey Bitch! Remember me?" He asked.

"Yes, Dicky, I remember you. The smell is quite unforgettable."

"Yeah that's right with that slick ass pretty fucking mouth. You better just shut the fuck up and listen up, if you know what is good for you!"

"Well, little Dicky, I have always felt that as a grown woman I could decide what's best or good for me. Maybe I should just get the Lua brothers up here to deal with you. They said you bounce off of things pretty nicely. You remember the Lua brothers don't you Dicky?"

"To hell with you and your jungle boys. You better listen up like I said. You closing up in a few days, but you ain't reopening like you think. You're

gonna stay closed or else. I run Valleybrook lady. City council is mine. Police department is mine. I am Valleybrook. They're all mine, bought and paid for bitch."

"Well, Dicky, are you finished? It's time for you to go!" I picked up the phone. "I wouldn't be here when the Lua brothers get here." I said.

"Remember what I said. You stay closed you hear?" He said as he rushed out the door and down the stairs to the exit.

Dammit, this guy was really becoming a pain in the ass.

Gene asked, "What are we gonna do Boss Lady?"

"We're going to do exactly what we set out to do darlin'. You just let Boss Lady worry about that." And worry about it, I did. I thought about it for a while and then I snapped and did not hardly think about it again. We had a makeover to think about.

Chapter 39

With home life exceptional, and with Mary Anne and Dorothy doing a great job, I was really able to focus right where I needed to on the remodel. The last night open before the grand reopening, I asked the staff to all stay for a drink. All regular employees were given half wages for the month and asked to come back. Each of the twelve girls we wanted to return were given two hundred and reminded about the fifty per night bogie we were going to offer when we reopened. Gene and I thanked them all, and we walked out to the parking lot with them. Gene, Kris and I walked back inside.

"You boys ready to do this shit?"

They nodded yes. The three of us would be the whole staff for the next month or so. We were excited about this place. Our customers were excited about this place. Our employees were excited. Hell! I guess you could say it was exciting. This was fun. We had a shot of tequila together and agreed to take two days off. Then come back to work.

It was nearing Thanksgiving and Cassie had been bragging about her ability to put on a turkey day spread. Amy Jo concurred, lavishing high praise upon

her mother's holiday oriented kitchen talents. I did not doubt either of them. Cassie had proven to be a fantastic cook and I saw no reason why this would be a weak spot for her. In fact, for the first time ever I had decided to host Thanksgiving dinner. I was determined to give Cassie a big enough stage. Gene and Kris were invited. So was Victor. To round things out, Mary Anne, Dorothy and the Lua brothers were asked to join us as well. Everyone had accepted and claimed to look forward to it. I sure was.

I had always loved this time of year, and this year was not an exception. This year I had a family to share it with. After a couple days off we had a few days' worth of work to do and then it was time for Thanksgiving break.

After completely relaxing for two days, I called Gene and Kris. We agreed to sleep in and show up about one. I offered to meet them and bring the pizza. They accepted. I was ready to get back to it. They were too. There was much to do.

I woke up about mid-morning on the day that we were to reenter the closed for business club. I took a couple puffs off of a nice joint and took a moment to reflect on the coming month. The framing and reframing that needed to be done was complete. Structurally it was ready. We had narrowed things down to the contractors we were going to use. All the contractors were aware of the timelines and they all felt like our timelines were reasonable or at least mostly reasonable. My team and I would still have to be on

our game, however. I ran the next five weeks through my mind. Playing the plan through the fast forward of the day to day grind that would soon be my life. After a couple hours of this, I found myself laying there with a smile. I got up quickly, showered, put my hair in a ponytail and after putting on a running suit, I ran out to the Camaro to meet the guys at the club.

We weren't all bright eyed and bushy tailed, but all three of us were there. We sat down and began to eat some pizza and brainstorm. Suddenly my new best friend, little Dicky, stormed in smiling like the cat that ate the canary. The sorry mother fucker sat right down at the table, grabbed a piece of pizza and took a bite smiling.

"Have a slice of pizza, Dicky! What else can we help you with?" I asked, betraying the calm veneer of my voice with my angry red face.

"I will, thanks. You know I bet that I get your permit pulled. You should be careful spending all this money for a club you probably won't reopen."

That son of a bitch had now really pissed me off. "Do what you feel like you have to do little Dicky, and I'll do the same. Didn't I tell you before? You're no longer involved in the way this club spends money. Get out, please."

His sorry ass walked out laughing.

I had made an error. I had Kris call the Luas. They were returning to active duty. Now was not the time to be cheap. I had Kris begin to interview

additional security personnel. We were going to hire three more guys and retain them with half wages until we reopened. I was not giving this guy a chance to catch us unprepared again. Also, he would not win any more minor battles by distracting us from our primary field of focus.

Over the next few days Kris found the three guys we needed. They were all former collegiate wrestlers. They all had a clean appearance and mixed martial arts backgrounds. While he was busy doing that with Paulie and Kalo, Gene and I had confirmed all the little parts and pieces necessary to complete the task before us. Assured that we were as prepared as we could be, the five of us locked up and left The Lady for the Thanksgiving holiday.

Chapter 40

Waking up on Thanksgiving morning to all those smells was fabulous. With the smells of raw ingredients as well as the smells of partially prepared and some finished dishes. Oh my God, even if I had just eaten, those smells would have me hungry again. After a long bath I walked downstairs to find Cassie in the kitchen brewing a fresh pot of coffee. We each smoked a little bit of grass and had a cup of coffee with a cream cheese bagel.

Amy Jo and Colton got up around ten and I sat with Colton on my lap watching the Thanksgiving Day parade on TV. His eyes would get so big. It was as if they became more blue as he stared at the oversized images of the oversized sized balloons passing in front of him. He was surely my little man and he was having a big time too. Amy Jo watched the kitchen for Mom while she got more appropriately dressed. She and I shared easy banter on this first Thanksgiving for our little group. We found that we got along very well. I found myself very proud of her.

Not too surprising, the Lua brothers were the first of our guests to arrive. I should have known where food was concerned they were not going to be

late. First to arrive and last to leave was probably more like it. Then Victor knocked and I was happy to see him, as well as honored that he chose to spend this day with us. Right behind him were Dorothy and Mary Anne. Kris showed up with a cute date, which stressed out Amy Jo. I suspect that was precisely the desired effect. Lastly came my club manager and new friend, Gene. Our group was complete.

As we sat down, it awkwardly fell to me to say grace. I had never had this opportunity before and had I been asked before that very moment I believe that I may have shied away from it. Instead I found myself with sincere, appropriate and very grateful words coming out of my mouth addressing our creator. I looked around realizing that I was indeed thankful and had a room full of people that I could and should be thankful to have.

We dug in and it was quickly obvious that Cassie could indeed cook her little ass off. The food was amazing! The only thing more astonishing was the amount of food that the Lua brothers could consume. Which by the way could have only been described as otherworldly. I suspected that they held back to make sure the rest of us had food to eat. They paced themselves perfectly as the rest of us confirmed that we were stuffed. They emptied the remaining dishes. Thank goodness that the pantry was full. If we were to snack any later we would be leaning on it.

Several of us stepped out back to smoke a couple of fat joints and visit. We had eaten so much

that even this very kind bud left us with no munchies.
We lingered about, talking with each other, alternating
between topics ranging from the deeply intellectual to
the absolutely stupid. Whatever the topic we always
found some way to make it humorous to us all.

As we ambled back into the house we broke off
into little factions of Thanksgiving Day pleasures.
Amy Jo, Cassie, Mary Anne and Kris's date, Patricia,
began to play Monopoly. Dorothy who was quite into
Paulie Lua, was watching the Dallas Cowboys play
along with everyone else other than Victor, Colton and
me. The three of us lingered in the dining room while
Colton amused himself, sometimes at our expense.
Then Victor changed the topic to me.

He asked me about the club. He wanted to
know when I thought we would reopen. We talked for
a moment about Dicky Abner. Victor apparently knew
some of the fellows that were associated with him. It
turned out nearly no one liked him any more than I did.
From what I could gather that included his own kids.
We talked a little about the odd circumstances of
Ciara's and Andrea's disappearance. He gave me some
background on Dorothy and Mary Anne. We discussed
the massage company and my future plans for it. He
felt very open today, obviously, and he apparently
needed to clear the air as well as get up to speed.
Lastly, before we could just be two friends again, we
discussed my involvement with the methamphetamine
business. He wanted to know exactly how much longer

I saw myself involved with it, what exactly my goals were and where I was in relation to completing them.

Then he was done discussing such things and the conversation turned to things like the beauty of the wood used to manufacture the room's table and chairs. He let me know which pieces of my art collection he liked and which ones he despised. The ones left out of the discussion by default were the ones that left him indifferent. Indifference being the biggest snub where art was concerned by the way. He commented that he was impressed with how well I seemed to be holding up through it all. He asked if I was truly holding up as well as I appeared to be? He had become either an attentive and cherished friend, or he was the most diabolical man I had ever met and was setting me up for a ride. I suspected that he may be a little of both. I wondered if just maybe he was the most diabolical man I had ever known and that also he was a trustworthy friend who was truly attentive to my needs. Or could he merely be keeping his options open.

After the festivities were over Amy Jo and I had kitchen clean up duty by default. It was a chore, but it was somehow more fun than I expected. When it was done and all that was evidence of our labor was two trash bags sitting outside of the side door and the hum of the dishwasher, we lay down in our damp sweats, face up on the living room floor and fired up the first of a few joints as well as the first of a few bowls of meth. We lay there getting high, while we rolled around giggling, listening to, and watching music videos,

talking to each other and randomly commenting in no particular order and yet still no chaos. We were just comfortable and enjoying it.

Chapter 41

Both of us had been so busy with our lives that we hadn't been able to hang out like this very often. We were having a good old fashioned slumber party just the two of us and it was fun. It reminded me of the fun times I had shared with Katerina those many years ago and oceans away. I loved listening to the stories of her days at Norman High School. They were all still so fresh in her memory. She was telling me about a time when she was playing seven minutes in heaven with a boy who prematurely ejaculated when she barely brushed the front of his pants while enjoying her first tongue kiss. We both began laughing at the awkwardness of the moment. The laughter built as we were reminded of more and more adolescently awkward moments. I loved her stories partly because of the way she told them and partly because there was so little fun in the stories of my adolescence. In all the laughing and tossing around on the floor we found ourselves pleasantly, surprisingly laying one atop the other, face to face.

There was what seemed like a prolonged period of awkward anticipation as we stared into each other's faces. I don't think that either one of anticipated this.

We paused now in shock but, undeniable anticipation of what we must have both believed was a certainty. We both smiled, her down at me, me up at her. Then my hands pulled her face to mine. My lips were insistent before her gently determined tongue parted them. After a moment our lips parted for a moment leaving the both of us breathless with anticipation yet again.

The next minute we were each using our breasts, our thighs, our hands and our lips to explore the other. The attraction was magnetic and intense. There was no subtlety to it, none at all. Within moments the connection between us had exploded into necessity. The probing licks and hungry sucking that would occur next was something that had to happen. Our lust perhaps should not have shocked us but it did. We treated each other to delicious naughtiness and were each rewarded in turn over and over again.

We wound up naked and spooning the following morning in my bed. When Cassie found us while coming in only to inquire about Amy Jo's whereabouts, I was not sure which of the three of us was more startled. We all recovered and it was never mentioned again even though it would happen over and over.

After that moment, there was never an awkward moment between the two of us again. I was the first woman she had ever been with and even now, telling the tale, I believe I am the only woman she has ever been with. I hope now, as I hoped then, that I will be

the last woman she is ever with as well. That night, Thanksgiving night, was the start of the greatest love story of my life. It began also the relationship that I would give thanks for, many, many times over the years.

Amy Jo, Cassie, Colton and I got around and braved black Friday. We got a few gifts and wrapping paper. The real shopping on the agenda was for our tree and decorations. I had never done this and I was in many ways at the mercy of their customs and was glad about it. We went all out and by five o'clock that afternoon the inside of our home was transformed into a Christmas wonderland.

I was initiated into a family custom of theirs that evening. We watched "A Miracle on Thirty-Fourth Street" and "It's a Wonderful Life" on the night of black Friday. I loved it. I had never seen those films before and I had a fantastic time experiencing the huge range of emotions those films draw from mankind. I was both exhilarated and exhausted. My new girlfriend and I slept after.

I woke on Thanksgiving Saturday feeling great and spent the rest of the weekend doing all the wonderful things that I now associate with the Thanksgiving holiday each year. I slept in, fooled around, ate, overate, smoked grass, watched movies and played with kids. I don't know about you, but that's one hell of a list for getting one to feel thankful as far as I am concerned.

I woke Monday ready to get to work. The weekend had left me feeling gratefully vulnerable yet magnificently invincible. Funny how falling in love will do that to you. Isn't it wonderful? I got to the club early, made coffee and toast and sat there waiting for the gang.

Chapter 42

The Luas made it in first and they thanked me over and over again for Thanksgiving dinner. They got it on with Dorothy and Mary Anne Friday night. They started to comment on Amy Jo's ass when I interrupted them to say that she was off limits. They hooped a little bit and insisted on a fist pound. Kris walked in just before Gene. After we had discussed their sexploits over the holiday, we got some more work done.

The carpet and wall guys would be in shortly as well as the wood fixture contractor. The mahogany bar was in three forty foot sections and was due in two weeks. After all that, we had added more surveillance and more televisions, we would even have television in the bathrooms, 32 inch flat screens at that. The bar would have its face rocked in field stone. Then there was to be two new stages and additional mirrors and lights. As much as had been completed, we still had to take delivery of new furniture, ashtrays, glasses and liquor. The place had always had a liquor license, but Bennie the worm, never ponied up the money to get anything other than his case of popov vodka. What a cheapo!

We had a lot of coordinating to do and it was going to be hectic, fun, and worthwhile, as well as expensive. By not hiring a general contractor and dealing with all our subs ourselves, we had taken on all the liability for any damages during the remodel/make over. A lot was on the line and the last thing I needed was little Dickey Abner walking in.

Well that's what I got. Little Dickey Abner and his patchouli smelling ass. He sat down and said, "Remember what I told you, Bitch!"

It was a statement, not a question punctuated by the pistol he sat on the table in front of me. I was a little more than concerned, but was able to maintain my cool.

Kalo Lua approached and asked, "Is everything all right here?"

I spoke up. "Dickey was leaving. Please show him the door!"

I sat there fuming as I watched him walk out. This son of a bitch was way out of bounds. I was not sure what it was with him, but he was definitely trying to make up for something. I was not plugging into his game and after looking at the overall timeline for the makeover project I had decided that we would reopen on New Year's Eve with free champagne at midnight! Fuck Dickey!!

Back to the work at hand, the club. The subs came in and began to work. The space was all noise and bright fluorescent light, not the sultry demure low

light and intoxicating smells and sounds it would have when opened back up to customers. It did sound and smell like progress though. Progress is good.

Life over the next few weeks slipped into a really pleasant routine. Go to the club, run to see a few clients, go back to the club, have a meeting with the guys, go home and either place some presents under our tree or check to see if there were any new ones for me.

Once home I would enjoy the company of our little family group. Cassie was a great friend and that friendship continued to grow. Colton, my little man, was more hypnotizing than ever. As for my Amy Jo, she was intoxicating. There was growing an absolutely enchanting relationship. Ours was a connection that was painlessly comfortable with a subtle intensity about it. We were hot for each other and cool with one another. We were "peas and carrots" to quote a movie character that Cassie keeps talking about.

I had it all, home life, check; love life, check; work life, check. I was loving it too! I felt the respect that those around me had for me. I also felt the respect and admiration I had for those people as well. Life can be pretty good.

I also had money with a rebounding checking account, and due in large part to an agreement with Victor, my cash stores were in great shape. I had done some deliveries for him and was getting Dorothy and Mary Anne much more involved in my end of that game. As a result, my volume was way up and my

costs even lower than they had been. Victor was very impressed with "A Service for Men" and its ability to move ice. I had three hundred grand in box number two, a hundred thousand in my home safe, and after all the repairs would have a quarter million in the safe at work too. Like I said, life was good.

The only real problems I may have, center around "Little Dickey Abner", and I was not even sure what those problems were. I knew they probably did not involve the cops. The Lady would be run clean. I also had a few ideas on how to deal with him, and I had also begun to make those arrangements.

I had been out running errands one day. When I returned to the club, Paulie Lua let me know that Gene had walked out of the office three or four times looking for me. He had also called my cell a couple of times and was texting me as I was walking in. I had not gotten back with him since I was on my way to him. Now, however, I was wondering what in the world was going on.

"Where have you been?" Gene demanded as I walked in the office door.

"Look Gene, it's only been forty-eight minutes since you first called. What is going on? What's the deal, Pickle?"

"I'm sorry Petra. It's just that, well you will never guess who called."

"I won't have to guess if you will just spit it out!" Who called, Gene?"

"Billy Trent called that's who!

"Wow!" I responded. Then I sat silent for a moment.

William Clarkson Trenton, better known as "Billy Trent", was huge. He had a string of nudie mags and it was reported that he also owned about three hundred strip clubs in the United States alone, thousands worldwide. I figured that in that information there was going to be a big clue as to what the call was all about. I reached out toward Gene.

"Did he leave a number?"

"Uh yes. I have it right here."

He fumbled around on his desk and produced a card. It read Billy Trent, sexual liberator, private cell number 1-800-BIG-COCK. I laughed hard as I read it and began to dial. Apparently he had mailed it to me and it had gotten covered up in all the activity surrounding the club's face lift. During the call Mr. Trent placed to the club, he had announced and confirmed the envelope's presence. A voice answered the phone.

"Hello, Billy here!"

"Mr. Trent?"

"Yes, who's this?"

"Petra Novakova. I am with the "Platinum Lady" here in OKC."

"I know who you are. I would like to meet you the day after Christmas at your club Mrs. Novakova. Is that alright?"

"It's Ms. and yes that will be great. I will be in between 10 AM and 4 PM. Will that do?"

"That's great. See you then, Ms. Novakova."

The phone hung up.

"Well what did he want?" Gene stammered.

"I don't know for sure, but he'll be here the 26th. I guess we will know then." The two of us sat in silence for a minute or two. Then I said, "Well let's get after it. We have work to do!"

For sure, we did have plenty to do. Things were going well, actually, even better than that. However, if we weren't on top of things it could all still unravel on us. There was about one week to go until Christmas and most everything would be done by then. After the two day Christmas break, it would just be the camera and television guys and the furniture, dish and liquor deliveries. The buffet would arrive as well and we had decided to go with an all fried 6:30 PM to 9:30 PM buffet free with cover charge. It would also have one type of cake and a pudding flavor each day to boot. On opening night, it would be available all night. The plan allowed us to run a relatively small kitchen and still provide an easy, tasty buffet. We had a solid plan and with hard work and little luck we would make it.

Chapter 43

It was the day before Christmas Eve and the Luas, Gene, Kris and I were standing outside watching the sign go up. I looked over at them shaking my head.

"What's wrong boss Lady?" Kalo Lua asked.

"Well, Gene didn't follow directions now did he?" I asked with a huge grin developing across my face.

"No he sure did not, Mam, but he made the right decision though." Paulie answered for his brother with his big toothed grin.

There had been a couple of changes in the sign's design. I can say two things. One, I would not have agreed beforehand. Two, it was the right call to make and I am not just saying that because it cost fifteen thousand dollars.

The sign read "The Platinum Lady", a gentleman's club. "Don't you deserve platinum?" Wed.-Sun. 2PM-2AM.

Underneath it there was an area where black letter could be changed on a white background to advertise specials. Ours currently advertised our grand opening New Year's Eve and nightly buffet with ten-

dollar cover charge. The change was in the image. We had agreed on a cartoon strip type image with lighting that displayed hula hips. What was on there was a caricature image of myself in a black pant suit. It was great and the four guys who all seemingly had some part in it stood there very proud of themselves. I was proud of them too and I let them know all about it.

The whole group from Thanksgiving had been invited over to the condo for Christmas dinner and there were gifts for them all under the tree. I suggested that the five of us have a beer and one last stroll through the Lady before Christmas. They all agreed. As we walked in, I had Gene set the lights to the same setting that we would have during a business night.

The five of us entered from the entry way where the box office was together. At this point in the remodel, it was very easy to imagine what our customers would see and feel on New Year's Eve. All that was missing were tables and chairs, televisions and people. You could almost hear the music.

The burgundy carpet ran up the wall four feet high. The lightly stained flame mahogany border between it and the gold and platinum upper wall. The center stage with twenty-five-foot stripper pole. The VIP throne room for private dances. Each throne with its own stripper pole. The balconies had wonderful views. Even the mahogany rail felt like money. The guests here would be kings of their own little palaces, the dancers fantasy private princesses. We could feel the smooth electricity of the Lady's future as we

walked through. For ten dollars you could buy entry to the dream. For a little while they would become important to themselves.

We finished our beers and none of us found any deficiencies to mention as we walked to the exit. It was time to celebrate. It was time to enjoy the people we loved and to love those we enjoy. I hugged the guys and that was that. We had prepared well and we knew it.

I picked up some chicken for dinner on the way home. I was looking forward to getting there. I was looking forward to Christmas. I was ready for the feast Cassie would prepare for us all. I wanted to see the faces of my family when they opened their gifts. There was much overcome to get here. There had been much pain along the way. I had done such a good job of concealing the pain and now my life was healing it. I had known what it was like to love. Now I knew what it was like to feel loved.

The sex with Amy Jo was an intense and comfortable expression of the gratitude I felt for my life. With both of us concerned more for the other's pleasure and in the process of giving ending up with delightful receipts. Funny how generosity can at times receive a feast that would satisfy even the gluttonous. The rest that I received in her arms twice as deep as that apart.

On the morning of Christmas Eve, we three gals and our little man enjoyed the simple moments that make life the most memorable. Those little times that

bring unremarkable smiles that end up being the most remarkable of all. We lounged and laughed and helped Cassie with her prep work for Christmas Day. Before going to bed I took a last look at the tree. It was a great looking tree, but the presents underneath were even more magnificent. I went to kiss little Colton good night and smiled when I thought of his big blue eyes marveling at his first Christmas morning. As I joined my lover in bed, I couldn't wait for morning to come.

I was pleasantly restless all night and then my eyes found sunlight as they opened. Christmas morning was here! There was a stocking for Colton and a couple small candies and sweets. He also had a construction worker style high chair set. He went immediately to building some majorly important building and having a great time doing it. The three of us had even more fun watching him do it.

While he continued to use his Christmas sugar energy to construct one of the world's finest buildings, the three of us prepared for guests. With a background of Mannheim Steamroller, we got the food all ready to serve. Luckily we were finished before our guests arrived. One thing was certain, as they walked in they would smell a Christmas feast waiting for them.

Everyone came and had a wonderful time. There was great conversation and full bellies. There was giving and receiving and even though it is better to give than to receive it is best to give and receive at the same time. Everyone had fun and I was exhausted and ready for sleep by the time they all left.

Victor pinched me on the cheek and said, "It is a treat to watch you grow little lady."

As the last car drove away I became very aware that the next day would begin an important week as well as a very important meeting.

I was up before eight the next morning and out the door. With Billy Trent coming to the club, this day could be huge. This guy had mega sized financial resources. He had the ability to change our destiny at "The Platinum Lady". I was hoping his reason for being here was positive.

Chapter 44

I got to the club and made some coffee and waffles. As I ate, I made a list of things to check up on. We were still expecting several deliveries and we needed to ensure everything was on schedule.

At just before 10 AM the door opened and there was Billy Trent. He was wearing a peach colored Armani suit and white dress shoes. He fingers were as richly jeweled as Liberace. His long black hair pulled back into a pony tail. He was the perfect blend of tackiness and wealth. Somehow it still seemed sort of classy. It definitely was a softer appearance than my description belies.

He walked right up to the table where I was sitting and sat down. The two large black men that flanked him did not.

"Well now Darlin, judging by your appearance and the description I was given, you must be Petra?" he said questioningly.

I responded, "Yes, I am Mr. Trent. How was your flight?"

"It was a flight. It's my own G-five. Betta be good every time. Please call me Billy."

"Well Billy what brings you here?"

"To the point huh? I like that! The reason I am here is your club, its philosophy, its girls. I want to do a story and pictorial for Vixen magazine Petra. Also I am thinking about making you an offer for it. So there it is. That's why I'm here. What do you think?"

I paused for a minute. "Why? That's what I think I want to know. Why?"

"One reason is that we have mutual friends. The other is I need a property here in OKC."

"You can do the story for sure and you may interview and photograph any of the girls who are willing, but Billy you can't buy me out."

"Easy, easy there Petra. I only said I was thinking of making you an offer. Please at least hear it before you flat out refuse me. Would you consider a partner?"

"Possibly. I'll think about it. When do you want to photograph the Lady?"

"I saw your sign. How about a New Year's Eve story for the March issue?"

"Sounds great! Will you be here with us for New Year's Eve Billy?"

"Wouldn't miss it for the world Darlin! See you then."

He got up and walked out followed by his two body guards. I wondered who our mutual friend was. It also crossed my mind that it was no friend at all. If

all this was real, then this could really be big. Vixen magazine would mean a lot of publicity. A partner could also mean a lot of legal capital for me.

Gene walked in right after Billy walked out. He ran over to the table where I was sitting. "Well!" he said.

Being coy I asked, "Well what?"

"Well was that who I think it was?"

"Yes."

"Well?"

"Yes it was Billy Trent and he is going to be here New Year's Eve. They are going to do a big story and pictorial in Vixen magazine. He also is thinking about making an offer to come in as a partner."

"Partner? What about me Petra?"

"Who said anything about you? Tom, my lawyer, will be over later today with papers making you a one quarter owner of the Lady. So wipe that concerned frown off your face. This is a big deal."

He started grinning really big and doing the chicken dance in celebration. "I can't believe this Petra. I never dreamed."

He stopped and was staring wistfully off into space when I reminded him. "If you don't get us a club full of the hottest bitches, we will be screwed on opening night. So quit standing there star struck and get to work."

Work we did. Gene had put together what may have been the finest group of twenty-five women in OKC. He had great instincts and it showed in his work. All the furniture had arrived, the televisions and additional cameras had been installed. It was the thirtieth of December and tomorrow is the day. It was definitely the most important New Year's celebration of my life to date. The boys had just left and I was walking out to the Mercedes when a late model Monte Carlo pulled up. The window rolled down and there was that asshole, Dickey Abner, sitting in the passenger seat spinning the wheel of a stainless steel revolver.

He looked at me and said, "Remember what I told you Bitch!" Then the window rolled up and the car sped away.

The nerve of that guy! I was not stopping shit! He apparently did not know that this was not the first challenging moment in the life of Petra Novakova. Fortunately for me, Amy Jo was able to rub the tension, among other things, right out of me. I slept like a baby!

The big day was here and I was edgy as I woke. My lovely woman was kind enough to remind me that I did not need to be there until 2PM. Then she put a joint in my mouth and her head between my legs. What a lady? She was in tune with my needs. What more could I want?

The two of us selected our attire for the night. I wore a white Armani pant suit. She wore black. Around her neck was a lovely ruby pendant I had

purchased for her. It was almost gaudy in size, but not quite. The way it dropped into her cleavage and nestled there was absofuckinglutely divine. We both had on simple gold bands on our left ring fingers. Our matching French manicures looked great, and beaming with pride and expectations, I walked her to the Mercedes, and we drove to our, my, big night.

We arrived just before 2 PM and there were already cars in the parking lot. Some were empty, but others were full of men waiting to come on in. The air was electric and full of energy. As Amy Jo and I walked to the door we smiled at the appreciative wolf whistles and cat calls. We walked through the door and the Luas' chins hit the floor.

"Damn, Lady Boss, you and your girl are looking good."

We went up to the office and Gene was impressed with our appearance as well. "Ladies, you look platinum," he said with a huge smile.

"Are we ready? Is everyone here?" I asked expectantly.

"Yes we are. Kris is here, the Luas and two other security guys are all here as well. We have fifteen dancers here now and ten more will be here by 6PM. The hostess is ready to open the box office. The bar staff and waitresses are here. The buffet has enough food to get started. Two more guards will be here at 6 when the other girls get here. Am I missing anything?"

I smiled and said, "I think you have it under control. Let's turn on the lights and open the doors. Amy, baby do you want to man the lobby with me and greet our customers?"

She nodded and the three of us took off to begin the evening.

Chapter 45

Gene hit the breaker box and the club came to life. He hit the switch and the sign lit up. Before we knew it we had customers walking in the door ready to party. Amy Jo and I shook hands and wished our customers a Happy New Year. To my surprise within fifteen minutes we already had one hundred customers and dancers intermingling with big smiles on their faces and drinks on the way.

The place had even more class and energy than I thought it would. I thought to myself how nice it is when a thing exceeds your expectations. This place was awesome. A few of the girls took advantage of the fun kind of sexy that a costume could add. We had Bo Peep. We had Red Riding Hood and there was a hot as hell Elvira type in a white skirt and blazer with a little sailor hat that was fucking smoking hot.

Security, waitresses, customers and dancers all mingling and mixing with no problems at all. The waitresses were busy; therefore, we were making money. The VIP room was busy so we were making money, and the girls were making money as well. The two center balconies were reserved for Billy Trent and his guests. A smaller balcony was reserved for me and

my guests. There were one hundred twenty-five bottles of champagne on ice. It was really turning into a success. I was pleased.

We moved around observing the crowd as it grew and grew to near capacity. We would migrate back to the foyer periodically to shake hands and greet customers. As we walked into the entry way around 6PM I saw Victor just as he walked in the door.

He saw me first and spoke, "Ah ladies you are magnificent looking this evening. Do I get a personal tour?"

I was glad to see my friend. "You bet you can Victor. Come on in my friend." I motioned to the hostess and said, "No cover here. This man is my guest."

The three of us walked around the facility ending up in the balconies. Since we were upstairs, I suggested that we have a drink in my office. After Amy Jo and Victor agreed we sat down in the office and I opened a bottle of twenty-year-old Eagle Rare Bourbon and poured us each one on the rocks.

"Well Petra you have outdone yourself. The club is wonderful. Mary Anne and Dorothy are coming by later. They will love it."

"You guys can use the balcony I just showed you. We may join you, but it's yours for the night."

After I finished, the office door flew open. It was Dickey Abner and four greaseball goons.

"I fucking told you Bitch!" Dickey said flashing his gun.

"Apologize you son of a bitch. That's enough!" Victor yelled with his thick Hispanic accent. He was visibly furious.

Dickey made his next mistake. "Shut up beaner. This ain't none of your fucking business. You spics piss me off. Guys watch him!" He motioned for his idiot to draw on Victor and continued. "Now Bitch!"

"Enough, you stupid idiot." Dickey began to speak and was cut off by Victor.

"I told you to shut the fuck up! Do you know a man named Dobie Walls? That is rhetorical do not answer. I already know the answer. Oh! I seem to have a little of your attention. Let me get the rest of it. But first get these fucking pistols off of me, you stupid son of a bitch. God you are stupid."

There was a sick look appearing on Dickey's face as he motioned to his men to lower their weapons.

"I need to make a call dummy. You stay. Have them leave." Victor picked up his phone and placed a call while a now white as a sheet Dickey motioned for his men to leave.

"No Bueno. No!" he paused. "Si". Victor's attention turned to Dickey. "Dickey Abner, I am Victor Diaz."

Dickey turned even whiter and his mouth flew open.

"This is your lucky day Dickey. You are one of only a very few people who have spoken to me the way you have and gotten to live, at least for a while. You may thank Dobie. He says he needs you. I say you are too stupid to be needed by anyone, but I will let him have his way. Petra is my friend. She told me about your visits. We both hoped that you were smart enough to stay away. Of course, we have seen how stupid you are." Victor paused, maybe for effect, but I think it was out of disgust before he sighed and then continued.

"You may now hit your knees and pledge allegiance to this woman and beg her for her forgiveness. If she ever calls on you, you will help her. Do you understand?"

Dickey nodded as he hit his knees and begged at my feet.

Victor continued, "We have taken the recording of one of your visits, Mr. Valleybrook, to the fine people at city hall. I do not think they appreciated you saying that you run this town. I think they were under the impression that they did. I made a fifty-thousand-dollar donation to the City in the name of Petra Novakova. Dickey you have a club open and one not open tonight, correct?"

As Victor paused Dickey looked up from my feet and nodded yes.

'Aha, I thought so. Whenever Petra says you can leave maybe you need to get to the club that is closed tonight."

I told Dickey he was forgiven and he then asked Victor, "Are you sure you don't mean the one that is open? That's where the New Year's Eve party is."

Victor smiled. "No, Dickey, the one that is closed is on fire. That's what the call was about. You better check it out. I do not think your friends at city hall will respond very quickly to help you."

Victor began to laugh his ass off and he said, "Run along little doggie. Run along."

Dickey ran out yelling and screaming. I collected myself, which took a minute. I looked over at Amy Jo who just then began to breathe. Then I began to smile big.

"Why you Wiley old fox, you are my friend aren't you?"

He stopped laughing and said, "Yes your friend. Si, I am Zorro, the fox."

He started laughing again. Then Amy Jo began to cackle hysterically. We all looked to be cracking up we laughed so hard. When the laughter stopped or at least slowed down, my friend, Victor, showed he still had some tricks left.

"Let's go to the party and see if my friend Billy has come yet."

What a pal, Billie Trent was Victor's pal as well. I was ashamed that I had ever doubted him, even for a minute.

Chapter 46

We walked out into an awesome, awesome party. And party we did. Billy Trent had arrived and his photographers were taking photos. His writers were lining up a couple of interviews. Billy told Victor, "Thanks for the tip" and gave me a big thumbs up and an A ok. We all had a blast and toasted the New Year together.

Looking back on all of it now, I can easily say that the first thirty years was so very much more turbulent and violent than these most recent twenty-five. As I look over to the body on my bed, I have no regrets. She has been my lover for two and one half decades now and Amy Jo can still turn heads. As for me, I am not what I once was to look at, but as they say the older the violin the sweeter the music. For a gal in her mid-fifties I am still looking pretty good. Besides wealth can make up for a lot and I am wealthy.

That New Year's Day was a big, big day for me. I never again had the displeasure of having to speak to Dickey Abner again. I heard that Dobie had him killed about ten years after that fateful evening. "The Platinum Lady" was a huge success. The story in

Vixen was huge as well. Five of my girls from the club ended up being big porn stars with Vixen Video.

Speaking of Vixen, Billy Trent was impressed enough that he offered a quarter of a million in the form of a cashier's check and a one quarter interest in Vixen Video on its start up for a thirty-three percent interest in "The Platinum Lady". I accepted, and the connection between the club, and the sex empire Vixen, and the even bigger empire it was to become was a winning combination. A winning combination that made me about a hundred thousand per month. Gene still runs it for our ownership group today and is a very rich man.

Kris and the Lua brothers all got involved in the porn business and became "Big" stars. Hey I like girls. Who knew? I still see them now and then. Since retiring as actors, they direct for Vixen. They still call me Boss Lady, but why wouldn't they. They still work for me.

Colton just entered law school at the University of Oklahoma after earning his masters Magna Cum Laude. Cassie still lives in the condo. We gave it to her after we moved to the Bricktown Tower penthouse staring eye to eye with the Devon Energy building.

Victor. What else can I say about him other than, thank God for Victor. Turns out he knew where Ciara and Andrea were buried in their car. He also made sure they were in contact with what they thought were hit men from Mexico City. All the phone calls sure threw the cops off. It was assumed all the calls

meant that they took off. I got some extra help from him because he respected me and was pulling for me. I in turn gave the massage and dope business to his girls Mary Anne and Dorothy. Amy Jo got her accounting degree and she now audits my various business interests. I am worth forty-five million now. After Colton graduates he will run it all. Amy Jo also is the director of a ten-million-dollar endowment, The Jakule and Kateena Novakova Foundation, that does nothing but fund charitable organizations that fight to end human trafficking.

Every now and then stories do have happy endings.

The End

From the Author

Human trafficking is one of the most heinous and vile problems that our world faces today. It is not just an American problem or a North American problem or a European problem. This is a global plague and a waste of human potential. This book is a work of fiction and almost never do these women that are sold into sex slavery even get to live, let alone prosper.

Awareness is the key! With our daughters and sons, the old phrase "it's ten o'clock, do you know where your children are" is more important than ever before and the stakes may be the highest they have ever been.

Our children are being ripped from their lives to become slaves. Didn't we settle this one hundred and fifty years ago? Our world is better off without slavery.

Stand up for what you believe. Before you do that, you must figure out what you believe in. If you don't stand for something, you will fall for anything. Speak up and be heard. Do it for these women! Slaves have no voice!

Thank you for reading my book and my letter.

Scott Christopher

Made in the USA
Monee, IL
25 September 2020